W9-BPL-505

Everything
is funny as
long as it is
happening
to some-
body else.
—Will Rogers

Edited by

KATRINA FRIED & LENA TABORI

Designed by

TIMOTHY SHANER & CHRISTOPHER MEASOM

welcome BOOKS

NEW YORK · SAN FRANCISCO

This book is dedicated to my father, who really knew how to tell a joke, and my mother, who knows how to take one.

Thanks to all those who submitted their favorite jokes for consideration, especially John Downing, without whose wit and humor this book would simply not have been as funny.

Published in 2004 by Welcome Books®
An imprint of Welcome Enterprises, Inc.
6 West 18th Street, New York, NY 10011
(212) 989-3200; Fax (212) 989-3205
www.welcomebooks.biz

Publisher: Lena Tabori *Project Director:* Katrina Fried
Designers: Timothy Shaner and Christopher Measom
Editorial Assistants: Bethany Beckerlegge, Walaimas Cherdmethawut, Lawrence Chesler, Jasmine Faustino, Jackie Finlan, Diedra Garcia, Christine Harada, and Nicholas Mancini
April Fools' Day Party written by Monique Peterson *Production Assistants:* Naomi Irie and Kathryn Shaw
Production Interns: Jean A. Alix and Arnold Schlegel *Additional Illustrations by* Lawrence Chesler

Distributed to the trade in the U.S. and Canada by Andrews McMeel Distribution Services
Order Department and Customer Service: (800) 943-9839; Orders-only Fax: (800) 943-9831

Library of Congress Cataloging-in-Publication Data on file.

ISBN 1-932183-01-9

Printed in Singapore

FIRST EDITION

1 3 5 7 9 10 8 6 4 2

Contents

Classic Comedians

Comic Essays & Letters

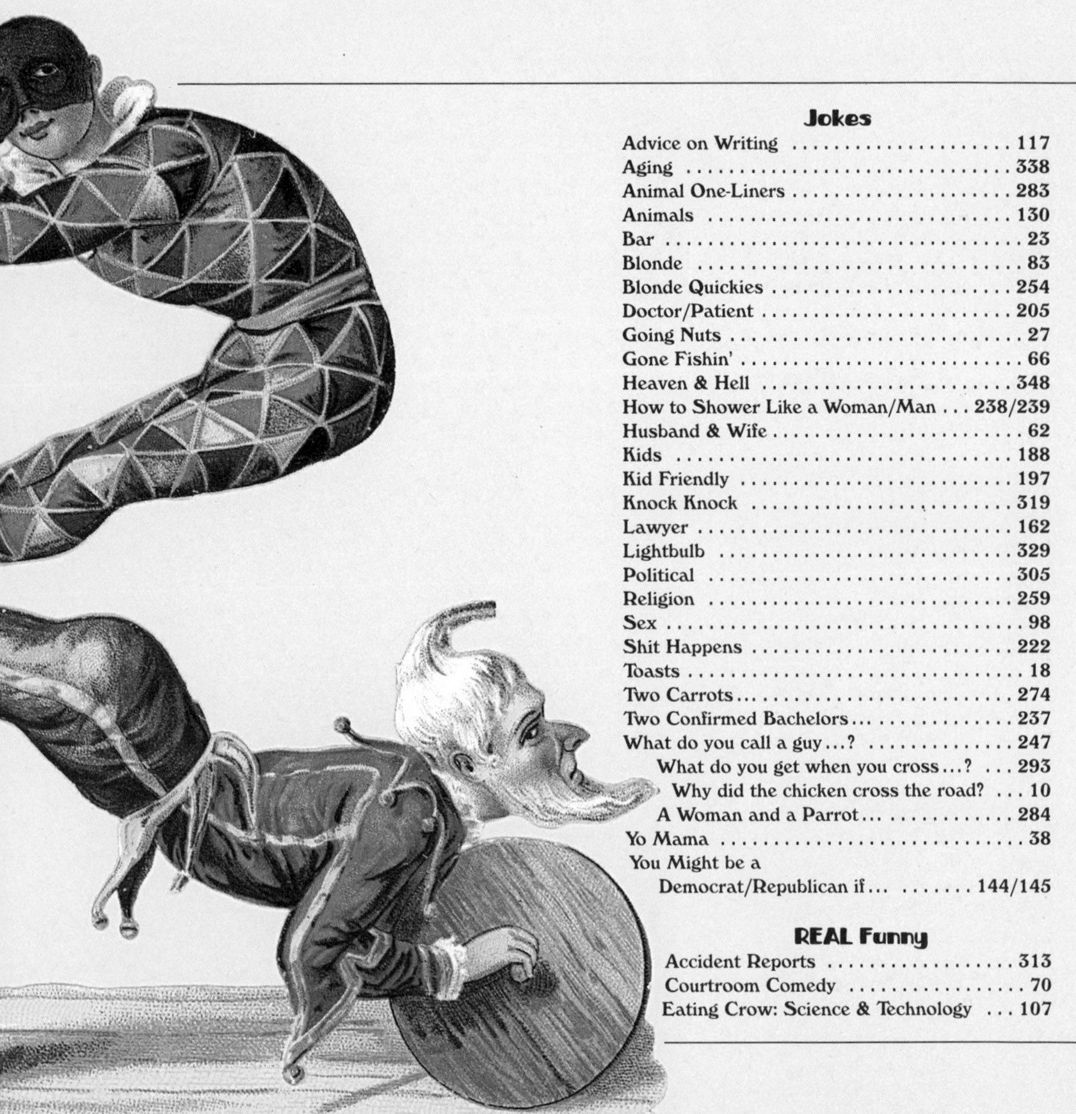

Jokes

REAL Funny

Contents

Foreword

The Five Golden Rules of Comedy

I owe every funny bone in my body to my father, whose dry, cynical wit was neither in the gutter nor near the brow, but somewhere perfectly in between. His unique sense of humor influenced the selection of every joke, pun, and prank contained in this book. Furthermore, it is from my dad that I learned the first three golden rules of comedy:

Rule #1: *It is just as important to be able to take a joke as it is to tell one.*
Rule #2: *The secret to a good joke is in the delivery.*
Rule #3: *Never pull a man's finger, no matter how nicely he asks.* (I learned this one the hard way.)

The fourth rule comes from comedian Woody Allen, who once wrote, *"If it bends, it's funny. If it breaks, it's not funny."* And it is true: The best comedy is a tightrope act. Lean too far in one direction or the other and you will fall flat on your face.

The truth is, either you know how tell a joke, or you don't. Either you can take a joke well, or you can't. *The Little Big Book of Laughter* cannot teach you how to have a sense of humor. But if you have one, I guarantee there are loads of giggles, snorts, and guffaws packed into the pages that follow. Thousands of jokes, limericks, puns, gags, comic essays, and riddles were considered and only the very best included. The content is paired with some of the most hilarious vintage illustrations you've ever seen, and the result is a truly unique comic anthology that entertains and delights.

What I personally love most about this book is that it is pure. Every page has only one intention: to make you LAUGH. It is one of life's most delicious and universal pleasures. For no matter where you are or what you are doing at any given moment, you would be better off laughing. And that brings me to my fifth rule of comedy:

Laugh hard, laugh loud, and—most important—laugh often.

Katrina Fried
Editor

If it bends, it's funny.
If it breaks, it's not funny.
—Woody Allen

Why Did the Chicken Cross the Road?

We don't really care why the chicken crossed the road. We just want to know if the chicken is on our side of the road or not. The chicken is either with us or it is against us. There is no middle ground here.

—GEORGE W. BUSH

Did the chicken cross the road?
Did he cross it with a toad?
Yes, the chicken crossed the road, but
why it crossed, I've not been told!

—DR. SEUSS

I envision a world where all chickens will be free to cross roads without having their motives called into question.

—MARTIN LUTHER KING JR.

In my day, we didn't ask why the chicken crossed the road. Someone told us that the chicken crossed the road, and that was good enough for us.

—GRANDPA

Absolutely 100 percent unsure.

—A BLOND

Only God knows.

—THE POPE

To boldly go where no chicken has gone before.

—CAPTAIN KIRK

For the greater good.

—PLATO

Give us ten minutes with the chicken and we'll find out.

—L.A. POLICE DEPARTMENT

Asking this question denies your own chicken nature.

—BUDDHA

To die in the rain. Alone.

—ERNEST HEMINGWAY

Could you define chicken, please?

—BILL CLINTON

The traffic started getting rough; the chicken had to cross. If not for the plumage of its peerless tail—the chicken would be lost. The chicken would be lost!

—GILLIGAN

The chicken did not cross the road. I re-peat, the chicken did NOT cross the road.

—RICHARD NIXON

Mmmmmm. Chicken.

—HOMER SIMPSON

To steal a job from a decent, hard-working American.

—PAT BUCHANAN

To cross the road less traveled by.

—ROBERT FROST

Because it could not stop for death.

—EMILY DICKINSON

Chickens at rest tend to stay at rest. Chickens in motion tend to cross the road.

—SIR ISAAC NEWTON

It saw Elvis on the other side.

—*NATIONAL ENQUIRER*

And God came down from the heavens, and He said unto the Chicken, "Thou shalt cross the road," and the Chicken crossed the road.

—THE BIBLE

What do you call a one-eyed dinosaur?
—*D'yathinkesaurus?*

What do you call a one-eyed dinosaur's dog?
—*D'yathinkesaurus Rex.*

What happened when the butcher backed up into the meat grinder?
—*He got a little behind in his work.*

What kind of blood type does a pessimist have?
—*B-negative.*

What happened to the cannibals who ate a missionary?
—*They got a taste of religion.*

What do you call Santa's helpers?
—*Subordinate Clauses.*

What do you call a retired comedian from Richmond, VA?
—*A Virginia ham.*

When should condoms be used?
—*On every conceivable occasion.*

What happened when it rained cats and dogs?
—*There were poodles all over the road.*

What do you call a chicken crossing the road?

—Poultry in motion.

Reflections on
Ice-Breaking
Ogden Nash
Candy
is Dandy
But liquor
is Quicker.

classic Comics

A rich man is nothing but a poor man with money. All the men in my family were bearded, and most of the women. Anything worth having is worth cheating for. Everything I do is either illegal, immoral, or fattening. Hollywood is the gold cap on a tooth that should have been pulled out years ago. How well I remember my first encounter with The Devil's Brew. I happened to stumble across a case of bourbon—and went right on stumbling for several days thereafter. I am free of all prejudice. I hate everyone equally. I never vote for anyone. I always vote against. If at first you don't succeed, try again. Then quit.

W.C. Fields

Famous for his raspy-voiced one liners and his love for liquor, stage and screen legend W.C. Fields rose from a hardscrabble life in Philadelphia to fame in Hollywood. He ran away from home at 11 and became a vaudeville headliner by the age of 21 with his hilarious juggling and pantomime act. His most famous characterization of a bulbous-nosed, beleaguered curmudgeon made him a hit on radio and in talking films, where Fields wrote and acted in many of his own movies. Starring in such movies as You Can't Cheat an Honest Man *and* My Little Chickadee *with Mae West, W.C. Fields displayed the inimitable improvisational and comedic talent that made him an American icon.*

Classic Comics

There's no use being a damn fool about it. Now don't say you can't swear off drinking; it's easy. I've done it a thousand times. Say anything that you like about me except that I drink water. Somebody's been putting pineapple juice in my pineapple juice! The only thing a lawyer won't question is the legitimacy of his mother. After two days in the hospital, I took a turn for the nurse. Madam, there's no such thing as a tough child—if you parboil them first for seven hours, they always come out tender. Start every day with a smile and get it over with. The cost of living has gone up another dollar a quart.

FULL. HANDLE WITH CARE

A woman drove me to drink, and I'll be a son-of-a-gun but I never even wrote to thank her.

Toasts Jokes

To our sweethearts and our wives—may they never meet...

Here's to the good time I must have had...

To champagne—a drink that makes you see double and feel single.

Here's to that moment of sweet repose
When it's cheek to cheek and nose to nose
For after that moment of sublime delight
It's fanny to fanny for the rest of the night.

So here's to ________. Always remember that you are unique... just like everyone else.

Health and a long life to you. Land without rent to you. A child every year to you. And if you can't go to heaven, may you at least die in Ireland.

Champagne to my real friends, and real pain to my sham friends.

May your wedding days be few and your anniversaries many.

I drink to your health when I'm with you, I drink to your health when I'm alone. I drink to your health so gosh-darned much, I'm afraid I'm losing my own.

Here's to you

and here's to me,

Friends may

we always be!

But, if by chance

we disagree,

Up yours!

Here's to me!

On the breasts of a
barmaid at Yale

Are tattooed all
the prices of ale,

And on her
behind

For the sake
of the blind

Are the same, but
they're written in
Braille.

Laughable Limericks

There was a young maiden of Siam
Who said to her lover, young Kiam,
"If you kiss me, of course
You will have to use force—
But God knows you are stronger than I am."

There was a young lady in Eton
Whose figure had plenty of meat on.
She said, "Marry me, dear,
And you'll find that my rear
Is a nice place to warm your cold feet on."

There was a young lady named Rose
Who had a large wart on her nose.
When she had it removed
Her appearance improved,
But her glasses slipped down to her toes.

Three Irishmen
walk out of a bar.

Bar Jokes

Two ropes walk into a bar. The bartender says, "Get out of here. We don't serve ropes in here."

The ropes go outside and one says to the other, "I have an idea."

He ties himself up, messes up his hair, and goes back in.

The bartender says, "Hey. No ropes."

"I'm not a rope," says the knot.

The bartender says, "You're not a rope?"

"Nope. I'm a frayed knot."

Paddy Murphy walks into a Belfast pub, looking like he's just been run over by a train. His arm is in a sling, his nose is broken, his face is cut and bruised and he's walking with a limp.

"What happened to you?" asks Sean, the bartender.

"Jamie O'Conner and me had a fight," says Paddy.

"That little twit, O'Conner," says Sean, "He couldn't have done all that to you, he must have had something in his hand."

That he did," says Paddy. "A shovel is what he had, and a terrible lickin' he gave me with it."

"Well," says Sean, "you should have defended yourself. Didn't you have something in your hand?"

"That I did," said Paddy. "Mrs. O'Conner's breast, and a thing of beauty it was, but useless in a fight."

A horse walks into a bar. And the bartender says, "Why the long face?"

So there was this dyslexic guy who walked into a bra.

So a five-dollar bill walks into a bar. The bartender says, "Get outta here! We don't serve your type. This is a singles' bar."

This guy walks into a bar and has a drink. When he's finished he looks in his pocket and orders another drink. When he finishes his second drink, again he looks in his pocket and orders a third. This goes on for five more drinks.

Finally the bartender can't contain his curiosity and asks, "What are you doing? What's in your pocket?"

And the guy says, "It's a picture of my wife. When she starts looking good to me, I know it's time to go home."

A Jewish man walks into a bar, sits down, and has a few drinks. Then he sees a Chinese man at the other end of the bar, walks over and punches him in the face.

"Ouch!" the Chinese man says. "What was that for?"

"That was for Pearl Harbor," the Jewish man says.

"But I'm Chinese!" protests the Chinese man.

"Chinese, Japanese, it's all the same to me," shrugs the Jewish man and goes back to his seat.

A few minutes later, the Chinese man walks up to the Jewish man and punches him in the face.

"Ouch!" the Jewish man says. "What was that for?"

"That was for the *Titanic*," the Chinese man says.

"But that was an iceberg!"

"Iceberg, Goldberg, it's all the same to me."

Bar Jokes

This guy walks into a bar, pulls out a tiny piano and stool, and a tiny little man. The tiny man sits down, and starts to play the piano.

The bartender asks him "Hey, what's that?"

"A twelve-inch pianist. Ya see, I found this magic lamp, rubbed it, made a wish, I got a twelve-inch pianist."

"Can I try?" asks the bartender.

The man with the piano agrees and a minute later, a million ducks fill the room.

"Ducks? I didn't wish for a million ducks, I wished for a million bucks!"

"Ya think I really wished for a twelve-inch pianist?"

A pig walks into a bar, orders fifteen beers, lines them up and drinks every one.

The bartender says, "I bet you'd like to know where the bathroom is."

"No," said the little pig. "I'm the little pig that goes wee-wee-wee all the way home."

A skeleton walks into a bar and says, "Give me a beer and give me a mop."

A bear walks into a bar and growls, "I'll have a Bud . . . . . . Light."

The bartender says, "Hey pal, why the long pause?"

Going Nuts

A guy walks into an empty bar and takes a seat. Suddenly, he hears a little voice say, "Hey, you're looking pretty sharp today. New suit?"

The guy looks around but there's no one else in the place. He hears the voice again. "Seriously… you are looking good, chum. Have you lost weight?"

The guy looks around again and still doesn't see anyone. "Hello?" he asks. "Is someone speaking to me?"

"You bet! I just had to say you're a handsome fella!" A bunch of other tiny voices rise in agreement.

The guy suddenly realizes that the voices are coming from a bowl of beer nuts on the bar in front of him. He stares at them as the barkeep finally wanders over.

"What'll you have?" asks the barkeep.

"What?… Oh, a pint of ale, I guess," mutters the guy, still staring at the nuts.

He finally looks up at the barkeep drawing his pint. "Hey, what's the deal with these nuts?" he asks.

The barkeep shrugs and says, "Oh, they're complimentary."

The Pig

It was an evening in November,
As I very well remember,
I was strolling down the street in drunken pride,
But my knees were all a-flutter,
And I landed in the gutter
And a pig came up and lay down by my side.

Yes, I lay there in the gutter
Thinking thoughts I could not utter,
When a colleen passing by did softly say
"You can tell a man who boozes
By the company he chooses"—
And the pig got up and slowly walked away.

THE BIRDS AND THE BEES

Ellen Degeneres

Hardly a day goes by when somebody doesn't ask me, "Ellen, how can I explain sex to my children?" Unfortunately, it's always the same person who is asking me that question. He's the man who runs the cheese shop I go to—Cheeses 'N' Things it's called (I've always been afraid to ask what the 'N' Things are). Anyway, this man's only child works in the store with him, is in his mid-twenties, and from the way he handles a sharp cheddar, can probably explain more about sex to his father than vice versa.

Whatever the case, I'm sure there are many other reasonably sane people who are troubled by this problem. And the more children there are (and I'm not sure where these children are coming from), the more explaining about sex there is to be done.

By sex I mean, of course . . . sex. You know what I'm saying. There are many different types of sex, but for the purpose of this explanation I'm just talking about . . . you know, sex. In other words, you might have two consenting adults, a coconut, a pound of confetti, and a very thirsty yak. What they do may be very beautiful and spiritual and fulfilling, but it's not necessarily something you'd care to explain to a child. Okay, I think we've

D.

defined our terms, so let's get on with the explanation.

Okay then, what you've got to do is just explain sex simply and to the point. You just say, "When you get older you're going to meet somebody that you really, really, really like. Well, if you're lucky you're going to like that person. Maybe you don't even like 'em a lot, but at least they don't bug you too much. Or, okay, it's, let's say, closing time at the bar—it's really late and you've been knocking down quite a few Rusty Nails. And you know how the lighting is at those bars. I mean, everybody looks good. But then the next morning you look at the person next to you, and you're like, "Argghhhh! Help me!"

Maybe it's better to be a bit more allegorical. Tell a little story. You could say there's a Papa Bear and a Mama Bear. And the Mama Bear says, "Where is that Papa Bear? He hasn't been home in a long time. He says he's working late at the pretzel factory, but I don't believe that lying grizzly bastard." So she hires another bear to follow the Papa Bear—a Detective Bear (or, if you prefer, a detective goat—don't be afraid to add your own spin to the story).

Well, the Detective Bear shadows the Papa Bear for a week. Then he tells the Mama Bear that every night, after work, Papa Bear goes to the same hotel room in the Poconos. Well, Mama Bear decides that she's going to give Papa Bear a big surprise. So, she goes to the hotel, kicks down the door, and there in the heart-shaped tub, sipping champagne, as naked as the day they were born are... No, this isn't a good way either.

There is a big fat queen bee, and she likes her honey. So, she's in her hive and all these male bees are just buzzing around saying, "Oooo baby, I feel lucky tonight."

Or you take a big tub of butter, some milk, two or three eggs, a dash of vanilla... No, I'm sorry, that's not sex, that's my recipe for French toast. At least I hope that's not sex.

You know, I think the best idea is just to let the child watch cable TV. Or go out and rent *9 1/2 Weeks*. When I was in school, they showed us a sex education film about a boy calling up a girl on the phone and asking her out on a date. Nowadays, I'm sure they show *9 1/2 Weeks* or something starring Sharon Stone.

So, in conclusion, that's how I would talk to a child about sex. I sincerely hope that I've been of help. Excuse me, but I've got to go out for a short walk. All of a sudden it has gotten very hot in here, and I've developed a craving for French toast.

As you get older, the
pickings get slimmer,
but the people don't.
—Carrie Fisher

Classic Comics

I blame my mother for my poor sex life. All she told me was "the man goes on top and the woman underneath." For three years my husband and I slept in bunk beds.

I said to my husband, "Why don't you call out my name when we are making love?" He said, "I don't want to wake you up."

My best birth control now is just to leave the lights on.

I once dated a guy who was so dumb he could not count to 21 unless he was naked.

I told my mother-in-law that my house was her house, and she said, "Get the hell off my property."

I hate housework. You make the beds, you wash the dishes and six months later you have to start all over again.

A child can be taught not to do certain things, such as touch a hot stove, pull lamps off of tables, and wake Mommy before noon.

I don't exercise. If God wanted

Joan Rivers

A trailblazer for female comedians, Joan Rivers has been winning laughs and creating controversy for well over thirty years. After a rocky start in stand-up, Rivers got her big break when she appeared on The Tonight Show *with Johnny Carson. Known for her self-deprecating wit and snappy one-liners, Rivers is often the butt of her own jokes. Author of eight books, she has also hosted her own radio show and two television talk shows. Today, she is best known to many as the Queen of the Red Carpet where she interviews celebs and delivers her classic comic zingers.*

me to bend over, he'd have put diamonds on the floor. The first time I see a jogger smiling, I'll consider it. I wish I had a twin, so I could know what I'd look like without plastic surgery. Florida wants to change the state's motto to attract younger people. They're thinking about: "More than just a great place to die." You know you're getting old when you buy a sexy sheer nightgown and don't know anyone who can see through it! My body is dropping so fast, my gynecologist wears a hard hat.

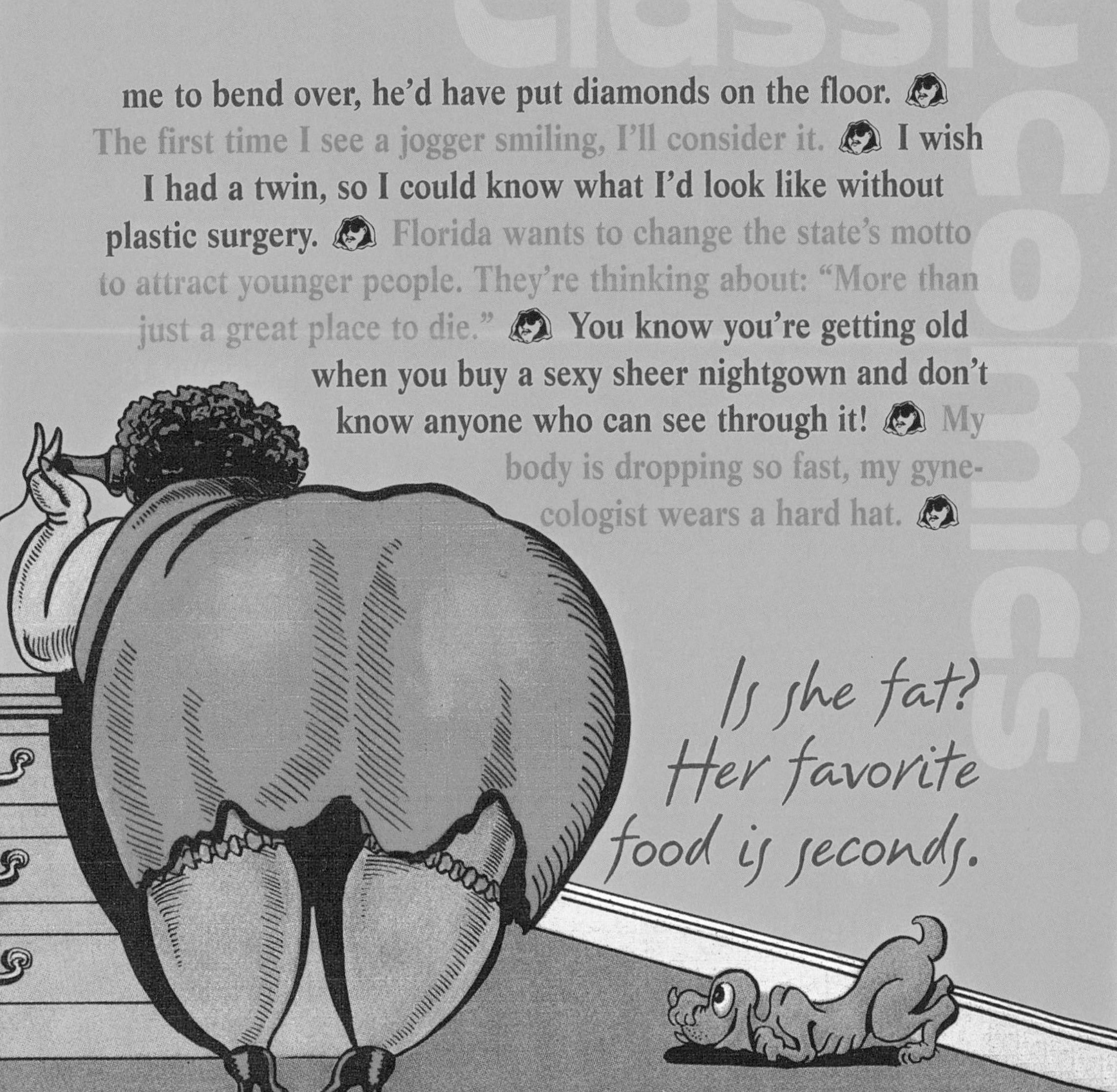

Yo' Mama's So Fat...

...she's on both sides of the family.

...she's got her own zip code.

...when she plays hopscotch, she goes New York, L.A., Chicago...

...a picture of her fell off the wall.

...her blood type is Ragu.

...she could sell shade.

...when she goes to the movies, she sits next to everyone.

...she walked into the Gap and filled it.

...she comes at you from all directions.

...when she was growing up she didn't play with dolls, she played with midgets.

...Weight Watchers won't look at her.

...she's got her own area code!

...she was born on the fourth, fifth, and sixth of March.

Yo' Mama's So Stupid...

...she looks at a can of juice for days 'cause it says concentrate.

...she thinks Taco Bell is a Mexican phone company.

...she got locked in a grocery store and starved!

...when she walked into Walgreens she said, "These walls ain't green!!"

...she asked for a price check at the $.99 store.

...it took her 2 hours to watch *60 Minutes*.

Yo' Mama Jokes

Yo' Mama's So Ugly...

...it looks like her neck threw up.

...when she was born, the doctor slapped your grandma!

...when she joined an ugly contest, they said "Sorry, no professionals."

Yo' Mama's So Old...

...her birth certificate says "expired" on it.

...she knew Burger King when he was still a prince.

...she walked into an antiques store and they kept her.

...when she was young, rainbows were black and white!

Laughable Limericks

THE FACE

As a beauty I'm not a great star,
There are others more handsome by far,
But my face, I don't mind it,
Because I'm behind it—
'Tis the folks in the front that I jar.

THE SMILE

No matter how grouchy you're feeling,
You'll find the smile more or less healing.
It grows in a wreath
All around the front teeth—
Thus preserving the face from congealing.

—Anthony Euwer

What do you get when you drop a piano down a mineshaft?
—A flat minor.

What do you shout when you drop a piano down a mineshaft?
—C sharp.

A peanut is walking down a street. Suddenly a man jumps out of the bushes, steals all the peanut's money and hits him on the head with a bat. What is the Peanut?
—Assaulted Peanut.

What do you call a bunch of grand masters of chess bragging about their games in a hotel lobby?
—Chess nuts boasting in an open foyer.

What do you call a monkey in a minefield?
—A Baboom!

What does a clock do when it's hungry?
—Goes back four seconds.

What do you call a pregnancy that begins while using birth control?
—A misconception.

What kind of doctor is a pediatrician?
—One with little patients.

What did one eye say to the other? "Between you and me there's something that smells."

What is black when you buy it, red when you use it, and gray when you throw it away?
Answer: Charcoal.

For answers see bottom of page 47.

Riddles: Logic

1. A boy is at a carnival and goes to a booth where a man says to him, "If I write your exact weight on this piece of paper, then you have to give me $50, but if I cannot, I will pay you $50." The boy looks around and sees no scale, so he agrees, thinking no matter what the man writes he'll just say he weighs more or less. In the end the boy ended up paying the man $50. How did the man win the bet?

2. Bill bets Craig $100 that he can predict the score of the hockey game before it starts. Craig agrees, but loses the bet. Why did Craig lose the bet?

3. Can you name three consecutive days without using the words Monday, Tuesday, Wednesday, Thursday, Friday, Saturday, or Sunday?

4. In olden days you are a clever thief charged with treason against the king and sentenced to death. But the king decided to be a little lenient and lets you choose your own way to die. What way should you choose? Remember, you're clever!

5. You live in a one-story house made "entirely of redwood." What color would the stairs be?

6. You are at a river. With you are a chicken, a bag of grain, and a wolf. You have to cross the river in your canoe but can only take one item with you at a time. You can't leave the chicken with the grain. He'll eat it. You can't leave the wolf with the chicken. He'll eat it. How do you get everything over and intact?

7. Two fathers and two sons went fishing one day. They were there the whole day and only caught 3 fish. One father said, "That is enough for all of us-we will have one each." How can this be possible?

8. If you were running a race, and you passed the person in second place, what place would you be in now?

9. How many flowers do I have if all but two are dandelions, all but two are roses and all but two are pansies?

Riddles: Logic

10. A woman shoots her husband. Then she holds him under water for over five minutes. Finally, she hangs him. But five minutes later they both go out together and enjoy a wonderful dinner together. How can this be?

11. A mother and father have six sons and each son has one sister. How many people are in that family?

12. How can you measure one gallon of water out of a barrel, if all you have available is a three-gallon and a five-gallon pitcher?

Answers: **1.** The man did exactly as he said he would and wrote "your exact weight" on the paper. **2.** Bill said the score would be 0-0 and he was right. "Before" any hockey game starts, the score is always 0-0. **3.** Yesterday, today, and tomorrow! **4.** I think I would have chosen to die of "old age." Did you? **5.** What stairs? You live in a one-story house! **6.** Take the chicken over first and leave it on the other side. Next, take the wolf across and leave him, but bring the chicken back with you. Next trip, leave the chicken where you started and take the grain across with the wolf. Finally, go back and get the chicken. **7.** There was the father, his son, and his son's son—two fathers and two sons! **8.** You would be in second. You passed the guy in second place, not first. **9.** Three flowers—a rose, a dandelion, and a pansy. **10.** The woman was a photographer. She shot a picture of her husband, developed it, and hung it up to dry. **11.** Nine—one mother, one father, six sons and one daughter. **12.** Fill the three-gallon pitcher and pour it into the five-gallon pitcher. Now fill the three-gallon pitcher again and use it to fill the five-gallon pitcher to capacity. What remains in the three-gallon pitcher is one gallon of water.

SPICY SURPRISE Unscrew the salt shaker and put a napkin over the opening. Make a slight dent in the napkin with your pinky and fill the dent with pepper. Replace the top and tear away any napkin that's showing. Now when someone uses the salt, it'll look fine through the glass, but only pepper will come out.

SHORT SHEETING THE BED Remove the blanket from your victim's bed. Undo the top sheet from the foot of the bed and fold it back so that the foot edge extends beyond the head about 10 or 12 inches. Tightly tuck in the folded top sheet and replace the blanket. Fold back the extra 12 inches of the top sheet over the blanket so that the bed looks neatly made. When your victim tries to get into bed they will find it impossible to straighten their legs!

SHAVING CREAM SPLAT! Wait until your victim is in their room. Fill an oversized manila envelope about three quarters of the way with shaving cream. Place the open end of the envelope under the door of your victim. Knock on your victim's door, jump onto the envelope, sending a splatter of shaving cream into the room, and run!

BED WETTER Wait for your victim to fall asleep. Fill a bucket with warm water and quietly place it next to the bed. Gently dip your victim's hand in the bucket and leave it there for about 10 minutes. The effect of the warm water will often cause the person to wet the bed.

SPILL TIME Take a plastic or Styrofoam cup and make a hole in the side right below the top edge. Kindly offer your victim a drink. Fill the cup with the cold drink of their choice and hand it to them with the hole facing them. The drink will dribble on their chest every time they take a sip.

BANANA SPLAT! Take a banana and squeeze it gently until it's very soft to the touch. Then take a knife and very lightly cut two or three lengthwise slits. Offer to get your victim a piece of fruit and gently toss it to them from a few feet away. When he or she catches it, the smashed-up banana will come squirting out all over their hands.

GESUNDHEIT! Cup a little water in your hand. Stand behind your victim and "sneeze" loudly. At the same instant, splash the water on your victim's neck. The gross-out factor on this gag is intense!

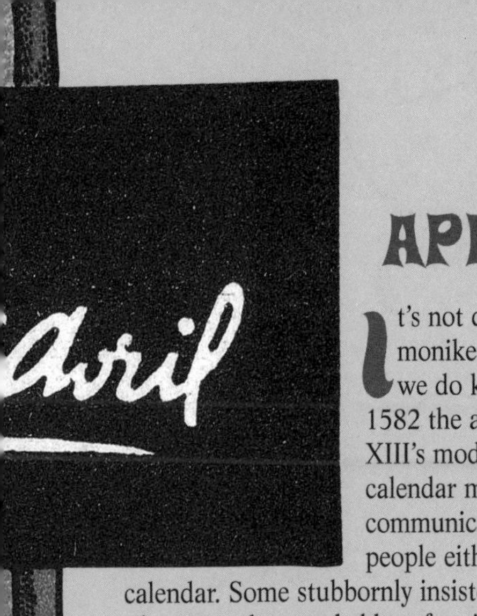

A BRIEF HISTORY OF APRIL FOOLS' DAY

It's not quite clear when April 1 received the moniker April Fools' Day (or All Fools' Day), but we do know the basic origins of this slapstick celebration. In 1582 the antiquated Julian calendar was replaced by Pope Gregory XIII's modern calendar. Among other changes, the Gregorian calendar moved New Year's day from April 1 to January 1. But communication was very difficult in the sixteenth century, and many people either did not believe or simply did not know about the new calendar. Some stubbornly insisted on continuing to celebrate the New Year in April. These people were held up for ridicule and soon given the label of "April Fools." They were given "fools' errands" to run and were subjected to practical jokes. This justification soon vanished and folks found any excuse they could to play tricks on one another.

The April Fools' Day tradition began in France and was known as *Poisson d'Avril* (meaning The Fish of April). As the gags spread across Europe and to the New World, a new spin was added in each place. Many famous pranks can be attributed to April Fools' Day, or to similar celebrations, such as the "kick-me" sign, resetting someone's alarm clock, or other such tomfoolery. Today we celebrate April Fools' Day by preying on gullible friends and family in silly, spirited fun.

April Fools' Day Party

Turn April Fools' Day into an event for the merriest of pranksters by throwing a party. Celebrate the sillies with everything from invitations and decorations to finger foods and fun and games. Encourage party-goers to come with tricks up their sleeves and see how many stunts you can pull collectively throughout the day. Have a ball, and remember… anything goes!

INVISIBLE INVITES

Let the fun begin with the invitations you send in the mail. These prankish postcards will set the tone for the event and let your guests know to bring a sense of humor to your party:

- Write an invitation in "invisible ink" on blank white paper by using a Q-tip as a quill and lemon juice as ink. Your guests will need to hold the paper up to a lightbulb for the words to become legible. Offer a hint on the back of the envelope, such as, "For a bright idea, read under a 100-watt bulb."
- You can also use white crayons on white paper to write an invisible message. In order to read the invitation, your party victims will need to rub a pencil or dark crayon over the paper to reveal the details.
- Print "reverse" invitations, so guests will need to read right to left and bottom to top to make sense of your nonsensical invite.
- Create a mirror-image message by writing your invitation on the back of a Styrofoam tray. Brush over your message with watercolor ink or similar water-based paint, then gently press a sheet of paper on top of the Styrofoam. Your message will appear on the paper backwards, requiring the reader to hold the invitation in front of a mirror in order to read it.

GET YOUR YUKS HERE

Keep a large "grab-gag" serving bowl or bag filled with joke party favors by the front door. As guests arrive, make sure everyone grabs a "gag" that can be enjoyed during the course of the party. Include items such as Groucho Marx glasses, Silly Putty, Pop Rocks, bubble blowers, kazoos, Super Balls, stink bombs, finger cuffs, mini joke books, dime-store puzzles, temporary tattoos, whoopee cushions, hand buzzers, Bertie Botts Beans, magic tricks, yo-yos, Mardi Gras beads, noise-makers, Bazooka Joe bubble gum, and the like.

TOPSY-TURVY TIME

Increase the giggle factor by turning your house upside down (so to speak). Rearrange furniture and household

items so that things are not where they ought to be: kitchen items appear in the living room, toiletries appear in the kitchen, bedding appears in the dining room and so forth.

- Hang colanders or frying pans above the toilet
- Place shampoo and shaving cream by the kitchen sink
- Store socks, books, stuffed animals, or dishes in the refrigerator
- String laundry in the dining room
- Turn chairs and tables upside down
- Decorate the halls with garden tools

PARTY FOOLS

Encourage partygoers to dress up in wacky costumes designed to get the loudest laughs. Offer gag prizes for the funniest get-up. Costume ideas sure to get chuckles include: dressing back-wards, funny wigs, jester hats, dunce caps, wearing clothes inside out, wacky ties, body or face paint.

Turn up the fun volume by dressing up a dummy or two. Stuff pants, a long-sleeved shirt, gloves, and shoes with newspaper or other clothing and use wire hangers and string to hold the "body" in place. You can create a head by topping a blown-up balloon with a wig, hat, and mask. Then situate your "model" guest in some unsuspecting place in the house. For example, you might direct partygoers to leave their coats and bags on your bed, only for them to find that "someone" is sleeping under the covers. Or, set up a dummy in a chair to look like someone deeply involved in reading a newspaper. Also, imagine the surprise of your guests when they go to the bathroom to find that there's a body in the bathtub or shower.

Funny Food

Spread some laughter with naughty noshes and crazy cocktails. Perception is everything, and the secret to fun April Fool's recipes is that things aren't necessarily what they seem. These mischievous visual and gustatory gags are sure to raise a few eyebrows and leave your guests in a titter.

CONFECTIONERY CAPERS

- Serve store-bought sandwich cookies, such as Oreos or Nutter Butters, but refill one or two cookies with toothpaste. If the cookies have chocolate or nougat centers, try refilling a couple with olive paste or liver pate.
- Just about everyone loves old-fashioned sugar cookies. Make a fresh batch that your guests will rave about, with the exception of one sourpuss who bites into the wrong one! Here's an easy way to plant the bait:

Fool o' Sugar Cookies

4 oz. (one stick) butter
2/3 cup sugar
1 egg
1/2 teaspoon vanilla
1 tablespoon cream
1 1/4 cups flour
1/4 teaspoon baking powder
1/8 teaspoon salt
1 additional tablespoon salt

April Fools' Day Party

Sweet Batch/*Fool's Batch*

1. Cream all but 2 teaspoons butter. Gradually add sugar and beat until light. (*In separate bowl, cream 2 teaspoons butter and 1 tablespoon salt.)*
2. In a glass measuring cup, beat egg, vanilla, and cream together. (*Remove 1/4 teaspoon from egg mixture and add to salted butter. Beat until blended.*)
3. Beat egg mixture into sweetened butter until creamy.
4. Mix flour, baking powder, and salt. (*Remove 2 tablespoons from flour mixture and set aside.*)
5. Add flour blend to egg mixture and stir together well. (*In separate bowl, combine flour and egg mixtures until blended.*)
6. Place teaspoonfuls of dough on an ungreased cookie sheet. (*Add Fool's cookie dough on baking sheet.*)
7. Bake for 8 to 10 minutes at 350° F.

Makes about 40 cookies.

Imagine your guests' reaction when they bite into one of these sweet-looking treats and get a savory shock instead.

Frosted Cupcake Surprise!

1 pound lean ground beef or turkey
1/2 cup seasoned bread crumbs
1/2 cup grated Swiss or Monterey Jack cheese
1/3 cup ketchup
1 large egg
1/4 teaspoon celery salt
1/4 teaspoon black pepper

Frosting: 3 cups mashed potatoes
food coloring

1. Heat oven to 375° F.
2. In large bowl, mix all cupcake ingredients until well blended.
3. Line muffin tin with foil bake cups. Spoon in cupcake mixture and bake uncovered for 20 minutes, or until cooked through.
4. Separate mashed potatoes into three separate bowls. Stir in a few drops of food coloring in each bowl to make yellow, pink, and blue frosting.
5. When cupcakes are done, top each one with a generous spoonful of frosting.

Makes 12 cupcakes.

Beverage Brouhaha

- Freeze ice cubes with plastic flies, ants, or similar bugs that can be purchased in dime stores or toy shops. Serve beverages on the rocks and wait for horrified reactions when partygoers realize what's in their glasses. Plastic frogs placed at the bottom of glasses work well, too.
- Serve tea and coffee with milk in an enclosed creamer. Put a drop or two of green food coloring in the milk to make it appear sour. Your guests might recoil when they see the color of their milk, but the jester java will taste just as good!

ALARMING SURPRISE

Set three or four portable alarm clocks to go off at various times during your party. Hide alarms underneath seat cushions and chairs or slip them in to various guests' coat pockets and purses. Then wait to see who jumps when the alarms go off.

BEHIND YOUR BACK

Before guests arrive, prepare stick-on notes with funny instructions that you can adhere to the backs of select peoples' clothing. Try planting some of these on your victims: "Tell me that I have food in my teeth," "Ask me about my new car," "Call me sweetcheeks," "Introduce me to someone I know," "Comment on my hair style." See how long it takes for people to figure out what's going on.

Jest for Fun

SLY VALET SERVICE

Offer to park cars for arriving partygoers. Before shutting off the engine, turn up the volume on the radio, turn on the windshield wipers, turn on the blinkers, and turn on the air conditioner or heater fan to surprise your guests with one last prank before they leave.

BOOBY TRAPS

Booby trap your house with some of the simple gags listed on pages 48 and 248.

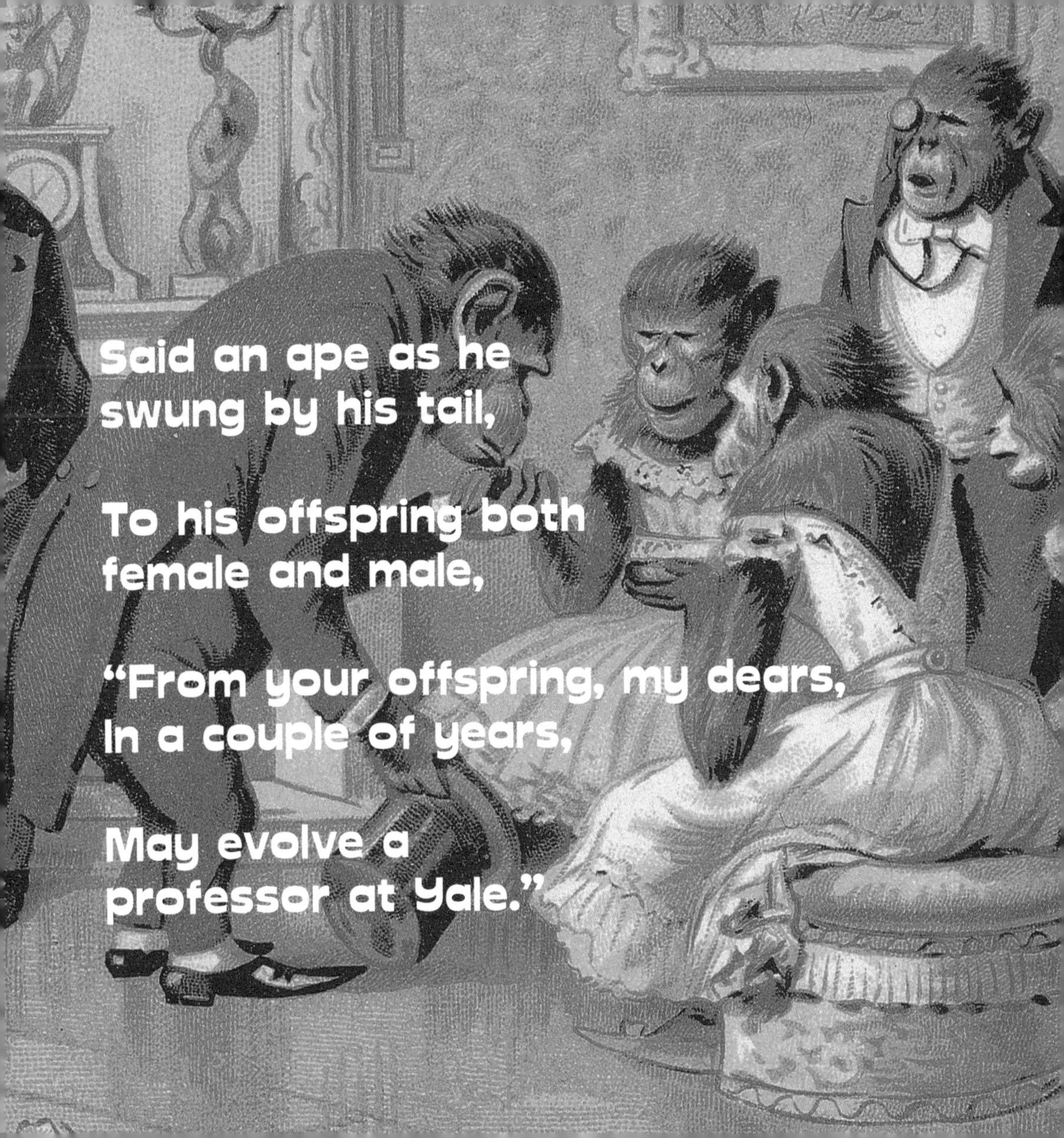
Said an ape as he
swung by his tail,
To his offspring both
female and male,
"From your offspring, my dears,
In a couple of years,
May evolve a
professor at Yale."

Classic Comics

A man's only as old as the woman he feels. Whoever named it necking was a poor judge of anatomy. I wish you'd keep my hands to yourself. I remember the first time I had sex—I kept the receipt. Women should be obscene and not heard. Marriage is wonderful institution... if, of course, you like living in an institution. Here's to our wives and girlfriends... may they never meet! Behind every successful man is a woman, behind her is his wife. Alimony is like buying hay for a dead horse. Politics is the art of looking for trouble, finding it everywhere, diagnosing it incorrectly and applying the wrong remedies. A hospital bed is a parked taxi with the meter running. It is better to remain silent and be thought a fool, than to open

Groucho Marx

With his signature bushy brows, painted-on mustache, stooped walk, and cigar in hand, Groucho Marx is possibly the most recognizable funnyman of all time. As the leader of the famous Marx Brothers comedy team, Groucho's hilarious wisecracking characters kept his audiences in stitches. Known as a clean comic, his one-liners were often full of sexual innuendo, but never crossed the line into profanity. A great lover of music, one of his best-known routines was a side-splitting rendition of the song "Lydia the Tattooed Lady." In the 1940s and 1950s, he hosted the highly successful radio and television quiz show You Bet Your Life, *and went on to make a number of films on his own, including* Copacabana, Double Dynamite, A Girl in Every Port, *and* Skidoo.

Classic Comic

your mouth and remove all doubt. Quote me as saying I was misquoted. Room service? Send up a larger room. Time flies like an arrow. Fruit flies like a banana. I never forget a face, but in your case I'll be glad to make an exception. Those are my principles. If you don't like them I have others.

I don't care to belong to a club that accepts people like me as members.

First Man: "So you married for money?" Second Man: "If I did, I earned it."

A woman was really letting her husband have it saying, "You're an idiot. You always were an idiot. You'll always be an idiot. If they had an idiot contest, you'd come in second."

"Why would I come in second?" he asked.

"Because you're an idiot!"

A farmer gets sent to jail, and his wife is trying to hold the farm together until her husband gets out. She's not, however, very good at farm work, so she writes a letter to him in jail: "Dear Sweetheart, I want to plant the potatoes. When is the best time to do it?"

The farmer writes back: "Honey, don't go near that field. That's where all my guns are buried."

But, because he is in jail all of

But, because he is in jail all of the farmer's mail is censored. So when the sheriff and his deputies read this, they all run out to the farm and dig up the entire potato field looking for guns. After two full days of digging, they don't find one single weapon.

The farmer then writes to his wife: "Honey, now is when you should plant the potatoes."

Two guys are moving about in a supermarket when their carts collide. One says to the other, "Excuse me, but I'm looking for my wife."

"What a coincidence, so am I, and I'm getting a little desperate."

"Well, maybe I can help you. What does your wife look like?"

"She's tall, with dark hair, long legs, firm boobs, and a tight butt. What's your wife look like?"

"Never mind, let's look for yours!"

After the annual office Christmas party, Perkins woke up with a pounding headache, cotton-mouthed, and utterly unable to recall the events of the night before. After a trip to the bathroom he was able to make his way downstairs, where his wife put some coffee in front of him.

"Louise," he moaned, "tell me what went on last night. Was it as bad as I think?"

"Even worse," she assured him, her voice dripping with disgust. "You made a complete joke of yourself, annoyed the entire board of directors, and insulted the president of the company to his face."

"He's a jerk–piss on him."

"You did," Louise informed him. "And he fired you."

"Well screw him," retorted Perkins feebly.

"I did. You're back at work on Monday."

A man leaves a bar, drunk as a skunk, and wisely decides that since he's in no shape to drive, he'll leave his car parked in the lot and walk home. As he's stumbling along, a policeman stops him.

"What are you doing wandering around out here at 2 A.M.?" asks the officer suspiciously.

"I'm going to a lecture," slurs the man.

"And who is going to give a lecture at this hour?" the cop asked.

"My wife," said the man.

A man comes home from an exhausting day at work, plops down on the couch in front of the television, and tells his wife, "Get me a beer before it starts."

The wife sighs and gets him a beer. Minutes later, he says, "Get me another beer before it starts."

She looks cross, but fetches another beer and slams it down next to him. He finishes that beer and says, "Quick, get me another beer, it's going to start any minute."

The wife is furious. She yells at him, "Is that all you're going to do tonight? Drink beer and sit in front of that TV? You're nothing but a lazy, drunken, fat slob, and another thing–"

The man sighs and says, "It's started..."

A man took off early from work to go drinking. He stayed in the bar until it closed, and came home extremely drunk.

He didn't want to wake his wife, so he took off his shoes and started to tiptoe up the stairs. Halfway up, he fell over backward and shattered the empty pint bottles he had in his back pockets. The shards of glass cut up his rear end pretty badly but he was so drunk he didn't feel a thing. As he got undressed, he caught sight of his cuts and bruises in the mirror and patched himself up as best he could before passing out in bed.

The next morning, his head was pounding, his rear was aching, and he was hiding under the covers trying to think up some believable story to tell his wife when she walked into the bedroom.

"Well, you really tied one on last night," she said. "Where'd you go?"

"What do you mean? I worked late," he said, "and stopped off for a couple beers on my way home."

"A couple of beers? That's a laugh," she replied. "You got plastered last night."

"What makes you so sure I got drunk, anyway?"

"Well," she replied, "my first big clue was when I got up this morning and found a bunch of Band-Aids stuck to the mirror."

WIFFIE'S?

Gone Fishin'

A man calls home to his wife and says, "Honey I have been asked to go fishing at a big lake up in Canada with my boss and several of his friends. We'll be gone for a week. Would you please pack me enough clothes and set out my rod and tackle box? We're leaving from the office and I'll swing by the house to pick my things up. Oh! Please pack my new blue silk pajamas."

The wife thinks this sounds a little fishy but she does exactly what her husband asked.

The following weekend he comes home a little tired but otherwise looking good. The wife welcomes him back and asks if he caught many fish.

He says, "Yes! Lots of walleye, some bluegill, and a few pike. But why didn't you pack my new blue silk pajamas like I asked you to do?"

The wife replies, "I did, they were in your tackle box."

With my wife I don't get no respect. I made a toast on her birthday to "the best woman a man ever had." The waiter joined me.

I haven't spoken to my wife in years. I didn't want to interrupt her.

I'll tell ya, my wife and I, we don't think alike. She donates money to the homeless, and I donate money to the topless!

My wife only has sex with me for a purpose. Last night she used me to time an egg.

During sex my wife always wants to talk to me. Just the other night she called me from a hotel.

One day as I came home early from work, I saw a guy jogging naked. I said to the guy, "Hey buddy, why are you doing that?" He said, "Because you came home early."

If it weren't for pick-pocketers, I'd have no sex life at all.

Oh, when I was a kid, I was ugly. When I was born, the doctor smacked my mother!

I drink too much. Last time I gave a urine sample there was an olive in it.

Rodney Dangerfield

Rodney "No Respect" Dangerfield is a living legend in the world of comedy. Born Jacob Cohen, this bug-eyed jokester began performing in his late teens as both a stand-up comic and singing waiter. After years on the club circuit, he finally broke into national prominence with appearances on The Ed Sullivan Show *and conquered Hollywood with a string of successful movies like* Caddyshack *and* Back to School. *With a career spanning more than 65 years, funnyman Rodney Dangerfield has definitely found respect.*

Classic Comics

When I was born the doctor took one look at my face, turned me over and said, "Look, twins!" When I was born the doctor came out to the waiting room and told my father, "We did everything we could… but he pulled through." I'm so ugly… my father carries around the picture of the kid who came with his wallet. When I was a kid my parents moved a lot, but I always found them. I remember the time I was kidnapped and they sent back a piece of my finger to my father. He said he wanted more proof. And we were poor too. Why, if I wasn't born a boy, I'd have nothing to play with! I find there is only one way to look thin: hang out with fat people. Some dog I got. We call him Egypt because he leaves a pyramid in every room.

My wife and I were happy for twenty years . . . Then we met.

REAL Funny

COURTROOM COMEDY

Excerpts from actual court transcripts

Lawyer: What was the first thing your husband said to you when he woke up that morning?
Witness: He said, "Where am I, Cathy?"
Lawyer: And why did that upset you?
Witness: My name is Susan.

Lawyer: The truth of the matter is that you were not an unbiased, objective witness, isn't it. You too were shot in the fracas?
Witness: No, sir. I was shot midway between the fracas and the naval.

Lawyer: Trooper, when you stopped the defendant, were your red and blue lights flashing?
Witness: Yes.
Lawyer: Did the defendant say anything when she got out of her car?
Witness: Yes, sir.
Lawyer: What did she say?
Witness: What disco am I at?

Lawyer: Now doctor, isn't it true that when a person dies in his sleep, he doesn't know about it until the next morning?
Witness: Would you repeat that question, please?

Lawyer: Do you drink when you're on duty?
Witness: I don't drink when I'm on duty, unless I come on duty drunk.

Lawyer: Is your appearance here this morning pursuant to a deposition that I sent to your attorney?
Witness: No, this is how I dress when I go to work.

Lawyer: All your responses must be oral, OK?
Witness: OK.
Lawyer: What school did you go to?
Witness: Oral.

AND YOU SAY
ALL THIS
APPENED
A CANOE
?
?!

Judge: Well, sir, I have reviewed this case and I've decided to give your wife $775 a week.
Husband: That's fair, Your Honor. I'll try to send her a few bucks myself.

Lawyer: Are you sexually active?
Witness: No, I just lie there.

Lawyer: So the date of conception of (the baby) was August 8th?
Witness: Yes.
Lawyer: And what were you doing at that time?
Witness: I resent that question.

Lawyer: Any suggestions as to what prevented this from being a murder trial instead of an attempted murder trial?
Witness: The victim lived.

Lawyer: Doctor, before you performed the autopsy, did you check for pulse?
Witness: No.
Lawyer: Did you check for blood pressure?
Witness: No.
Lawyer: Did you check for breathing?
Witness: No.
Lawyer: So, then it is possible that the patient was alive when you began the autopsy?
Witness: No.
Lawyer: How can you be so sure, Doctor?
Witness: Because his brain was sitting on my desk in a jar.
Lawyer: But could the patient have still been alive nevertheless?
Witness: Yes, it is possible that he could have been alive and practicing law somewhere.

Lawyer: Doctor, did you say he was shot in the woods?
Witness: No, I said he was shot in the lumbar region.

Lawyer: Could you point to someone in this courtroom, or maybe yourself, to indicate exactly how close to a hair color you are referring to?

Witness: Well, something like hers (pointing to Counsel) Except for more cheap bleached-blonde hair.
Lawyer: May the record reflect, Your Honor, the witness has identified Defense Counsel as the cheap blonde.

Lawyer: What is the meaning of sperm being present?
Witness: It indicates intercourse.
Lawyer: Male sperm?
Witness: That is the only kind I know.

Lawyer: Okay. How much earlier had you used cocaine?
Witness: I was getting high all that day.
Lawyer: All right. So you were using cocaine. Were you free-basing cocaine?
Witness: No. I bought it.

Judge: Mr. E., you're charged here with driving a motor vehicle under the influence of alcohol. How do you plead, guilty or not guilty?
Defendant: I'm guilty as hell.
Judge: Let the record reflect the defendant is guilty as hell.

Lawyer: Well, our objection, Your Honor, and I want to make this very clear, is that there's a time that truth has to stop, and that time—
Judge: Why does it have to stop?
Lawyer: Because the trial has started.

Witness: You mumbled on the first part of that and I couldn't understand what you were saying. Could you repeat the question?
Lawyer: I mumbled, did I? Well, we'll just ask the court reporter to read back what I said. She didn't indicate any problem understanding what I said, so obviously she understood every word. We'll just have her read my question back and find out if there was any mumbling going on. Madam reporter, would you be so kind?
Court Reporter: Mumble, mumble, mumble, mumble, mumble.

On Taking a Wife

Thomas Moore

"Come, come," said Tom's
father, "at your time of life,
There's no longer excuse
for thus playing the rake.
It's time you should think,
boy, of taking a wife."
"Why so it is, father.
Whose wife shall I take?"

Classic Comics

I wanted to be an atheist, but I gave it up. They have no holidays. When I read about the evils of drinking, I gave up reading. I've kissed so many women I can do it with my eyes closed. What's the use of happiness? It can't buy you money. I take my wife everywhere, but she keeps finding her way back. My grandmother is over eighty and still doesn't need glasses. Drinks right out of the bottle. If you're going to do something tonight that you'll be sorry for tomorrow morning, sleep late. You can't buy love, but you can pay heavily for it. My wife and I went to a hotel where we got a waterbed. My wife called it the Dead Sea. Why do Jewish divorces cost so much? They're worth it. A drunk was in front of a judge. The judge says, "You've been brought here for drinking." The drunk says, "Okay, let's get started."

Henny Youngman

Henny Youngman, the self-styled "King of the One-Liners," kept audiences laughing with his rapid-fire stand up routines. Raising Henny in New York City, his father dreamed he would be a violin virtuoso, but Youngman was a better jokester than he was a musician. He got his big break as a comedian on the Kate Smith *radio show in 1937 and created a line of "Comedy Cards" that got the attention of Milton Berle, who became a lifelong friend. Youngman worked the clubs relentlessly during his career, performing a whopping 200 dates a year. He leaves behind volumes of jokes and books, and is celebrated as one of America's favorite comedians.*

Classic Com

I'm now making a Jewish porno film. 10% sex, 90% guilt. A woman says to a man, "I haven't seen you around here." "Yes, I just got out of jail for killing my wife." "So you're single …" I went to the bank and reviewed my savings. I found out I have all the money I'll ever need if I die tomorrow. My wife's an earth sign. I'm a water sign. Together we make mud. A car hits a Jewish man. The paramedic rushes over and says, "Are you comfortable?" The guy says, "I make a good living." I thought talk was cheap until I saw our telephone bill.

Take my wife… please!

TOP TEN CONSTRUCTION-WORKER PICKUP LINES

David Letterman

10. “Excuse me, would you mind brushing the sawdust out of my back hair?”
9. “Your skin looks as soft and pink as Owens-Corning fiberglass insulation.”
8. “Union rules, miss—I have to inspect your foundation.”
7. “You take my breath away, like that time I passed out in a septic tank.”
6. “Haven’t I yelled degrading comments at you somewhere before?”
5. “Ever seen a thumb contusion this bad?”
4. “I’m afraid of heights, miss—could you come up here and hold me?”
3. “I can introduce you to the other Village People.”
2. “Yo.”
1. “I’m 36 years old and still carry a box lunch. Doesn’t that make you hot?”

It was just
the other day,

In a fortune-
telling place,

A pretty maiden
read my mind

And then she
slapped my face.

FUN HOUSE

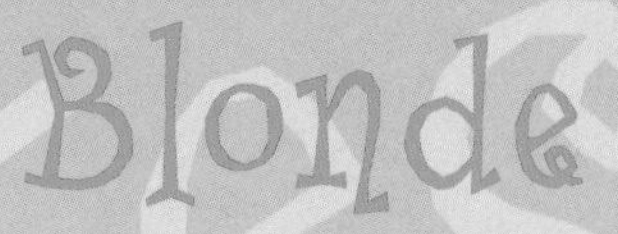

A brunette and a blonde who always drive to work together are running late one day. The brunette gets in the driver's seat and the blonde gets in the passenger's seat.

The brunette says, "I'm going to have to speed to get us there on time, so keep your eye out for the police."

As she speeds down the road she asks the blonde, "So, do you see any cops?"

The blonde replies, "Yes."

The brunette says, "Are they behind us?"

"Yes."

"Are they going to stop us?"

"I don't know."

The brunette says, "Well, are their lights on?"

The blonde replies, "Yes. No. Yes. No. Yes. No. Yes. No. Yes. No."

A blonde pushes her BMW into a gas station. She tells the mechanic it died. After he works on it for a few minutes, it is idling smoothly.

She says, "What's the story?"

He replies, "Just crap in the carburetor."

She asks, "How often do I have to do that?"

A blonde taking a walk comes to a river and sees another blonde on the opposite bank.

"Yoo-hoo!" she shouts, "How can I get to the other side?"

The second blonde looks up the river then down the river and shouts back, "You ARE on the other side."

A redhead walks into a sports bar at 11 P.M. She sits down next to a blonde at the bar and stares up at the TV as the news starts. The news crew is covering a story of a man on a ledge of a large building preparing to jump.

The redhead says to the blonde, "You know, I bet he'll jump."

The blonde replies, "Well, I bet he won't."

The redhead places $20 on the bar and says, "You're on!"

Just as the blonde places her money on the bar, the guy does a swan dive off of the building, falling to his death.

The blonde is very upset as she hands her $20 to the redhead and says, "All is fair. Here's what I owe you."

The redhead replies, "Honey, I can't take your money, I saw this earlier on the 5 o'clock news and knew he would jump."

"I did too, but I didn't think he'd do it again," says the blonde.

A brunette, a redhead, and a blonde are all about to be executed by a firing squad. The brunette is called up first. As the rifles are raised and aimed directly at her heart, the commanding officer shouts out, "Ready... Aim..."

Thinking fast, the brunette cries out, "TORNADO!" All the soldiers quickly scramble for cover, and the brunette slips away and escapes.

The redhead is called up next, and after refusing the blindfold, she watches in horror as the guns bear down on her. The commanding officer shouts, "Ready... Aim..."

Thinking on her feet, the redhead suddenly screams, "HURRICANE!" The soldiers all duck for cover and the redhead gets away.

Finally, the blonde is dragged up in front of the firing guns. As they raise their the rifles, the commanding officer quickly gives the orders, "Ready... Aim..."

The blonde girl suddenly yells, "FIRE!"

A blonde is terribly overweight, so her doctor puts her on a diet.

"I want you to eat regularly for 2 days, then skip a day, and repeat this program for 2 weeks. The next time I see you, you'll have lost at least 5 pounds."

When the blonde returns, the doctor is shocked to find she has lost nearly 20 pounds.

"Why, that's amazing!" the doctor says, "Did you follow my instructions?"

The blonde nods. "I'll tell you though, I thought I was going to drop dead that 3rd day."

"From hunger, you mean?" asks the doctor.

"No, from skipping."

A highway patrolman pulls alongside a speeding car on the freeway. Glancing at the car, he is astounded to see that the blonde behind the wheel is knitting! Realizing that she is oblivious to his flashing lights and siren, the trooper cranks down his window, turns on his bullhorn and yells out, "PULL OVER!"

"NO!" the blonde yells back, "IT'S A SCARF!"

A blonde, a brunette, and a redhead are stuck on an island. For many years they live there, and one day a magic lamp washes ashore. They rub it and, sure enough, out comes a genie.

The genie says, "Since I can give out only three wishes, you may each have one."

So the brunette goes first: "I have been stuck here for years, I miss my family and my husband and my life—I just want to go home."

POOF, she is gone.

The redhead makes her wish: "This place sucks, I want to go home, too."

POOF, she is gone.

The blonde starts crying uncontrollably.

The genie asks, "What is the matter?"

The blonde says, "I just wish my friends would come back."

A cute debutante
from St. Paul

Wore a newspaper
dress to a ball.

The dress
caught on fire,

And burnt
her entire

Front page,
sporting section
and all.

Laughable Limericks

A mouse in her room woke Miss Doud
Who was frightened and screamed very loud
Then a happy thought hit her
So to scare off the critter
She sat up in bed and just meowed.

A canner exceedingly canny
One morning remarked to his granny
A canner can can
Anything that he can
But a canner can't can a can, can he?

If you find for your verse there's no call,
And you can't afford paper at all,
For the poet true born,
However forlorn,
There's always the lavatory wall.

REAL Funny

EXTRA! EXTRA!
Real headlines published in US newspapers and magazines

Infertility Unlikely To Be Passed On
—*Montgomery Advertiser*

'Light' Meals Are Lower In Fat, Calories
—*Huntington Herald-Dispatch*

Joint Committee Investigates Marijuana Use
—A local newspaper in a suburb of Toronto

Tiger Woods Plays with own Balls, Nike Says
—AP Wire

Man Shoots Neighbor With Machete
—*The Miami Herald*

Economist Uses Theory To Explain Economy
—*Collinsville Herald-Journal*

Court Rules Boxer Shorts Are Indeed Underwear
—*Journal of Commerce*

Body Search Reveals $4,000 in Crack
—*Jackson Citizen-Patriot, Michigan*

Hospitals are Sued by 7 Foot Doctors
—*Providence Journal*

Messiah Climaxes In Chorus of Hallelujahs
—*The Anchorage, Alaska Times*

Sadness is No. 1 Reason Men and Women Cry
—*Omaha World Herald*

Study Finds Sex, Pregnancy Link
—CORNELL DAILY SUN

ARRIVED SAFE
A FLYING TR

Said an ovum one
night to a sperm,
"You're a
very attractive
young germ.
Come join me,
my sweet,
Let our
nuclei meet,
And in nine months we'll
both come to term."
AFTER
?!

Symptom Recital

Dorothy Parker

I do not like my state of mind;
I'm bitter, querulous, unkind.
I hate my legs, I hate my hands,
I do not yearn for lovelier lands.
I dread the dawn's recurrent light;
I hate to go to bed at night.
I snoot at simple, earnest folk.
I cannot take the gentlest joke.
I find no peace in paint or type.
My world is but a lot of tripe.
I'm disillusioned, empty-breasted.
For what I think, I'd be arrested.
I am not sick, I am not well.
My quondam dreams are shot to hell.
My soul is crushed, my spirit sore;
I do not like me anymore.
I cavil, quarrel, grumble, grouse.
I ponder on the narrow house.
I shudder at the thought of men.
I'm due to fall in love again.

When you're in love, it's the most glorious two and a half days of your life.
—Richard Lewis

REAL Funny

KIDS ON LOVE

Real statements made by children on the subject of love

"No one is sure why [love] happens, but I heard it has something to do with how you smell... That's why perfume and deodorant are so popular."

—Mae, age 9

"Love will find you, even if you are trying to hide from it. I've been trying to hide from it since I was five, but the girls keep finding me."

—Dave, age 8

"When a person gets kissed for the first time, they fall down and they don't get up for at least an hour."

—Wendy, age 8

"One of you should know how to write a check. Because, even if you have tons of love, there is still going to be a lot of bills."

—Ava, age 8

"Love is the most important thing in the world, but baseball is good too."

—Greg, age 8

"Twenty-three is the best age [to fall in love] because you will have known the person FOREVER by then."

—Camille, age 10

"It's better for girls to be single but not for boys. Boys need someone to clean up after them."

—Anita, age 9

On how to make someone fall in love with you:

"Tell them that you own a whole bunch of candy stores."

—Del, age 6

"Shake your hips and hope for the best."

—Camille, age 9

"One way is to take the girl out to eat. Make sure it's something she likes to eat. French fries usually works for me."

— Bart, age 9

"Tell [her] that she looks pretty even if she looks like a truck."

—Ricky, age 10

"It isn't always just how you look. Look at me. I'm handsome like and I haven't got anybody to marry me yet."
—Brian, age 7

Sex Jokes

In a G-rated movie, the boy gets the girl. In an R-rated movie, the bad guy gets the girl. In X-rated pictures, everybody gets the girl.

A chicken and an egg are lying in bed. The chicken is leaning against the headboard smoking a cigarette, with a satisfied smile on its face. The egg, looking a bit pissed off, grabs the sheet, rolls over, and says, "Well, I guess we finally answered THAT question."

Two golfers are waiting their turn on the tee, when a naked woman runs across the fairway and into the woods. Two men in white coats, and another guy carrying two buckets of sand are chasing her, and a little old man is bringing up the rear.

One of the golfers asks the old man, "What the hell is going on?"

The old guy says, "She's a nymphomaniac from the asylum, she keeps trying to escape, and us attendants are trying to catch her."

The golfer says, "What about the guy with the buckets of sand?"

The old guy says, "That's his handicap. He caught her last time."

A young married couple vowed to each other that whoever died first would contact the other and tell them what the afterlife was like. Many years later, the husband died of a heart attack, and true to his promise, contacted his wife.

TOMORROW, CADDY, I'M GOING AROUND IN LESS!
SCORE CARD

EXTRA

"Martha, this is John. Can you hear me?"

"Yes John," answered Martha tearfully. "Tell me, what is it like where you are?"

"It's beautiful. There are blue skies, a soft breeze, and it's almost always sunny."

"What do you do all day?" asked Martha.

"Well, we get up before sunrise, have a good breakfast, and make love until noon. Then we have lunch and nap until two. Then we make love again until about five. After dinner, we go at it again until we fall asleep and when we wake up the next morning we start all over again."

"Oh, Fred," says Martha," Heaven sounds like a wonderful place!"

"Heaven? Who said anything about Heaven? I'm a rabbit in Arizona!"

A little girl and a little boy are arguing about who's better—boys or girls. Each believes that their sex is superior. Finally, the boy drops his pants and says, "Here's something I have that you'll never have!"

The little girl is pretty upset by this, since it is quite clearly true. She turns and runs home.

A while later, she comes skipping back with a smile on her face. The boys asks her why she's so happy. So she drops her pants, and says, "My mommy says that with one of these, I can have as many of those as I want!"

To err is human, but it feels divine. When choosing between two evils I like to try the one I've never tried before. I generally avoid temptation unless I can't resist it. I used to be Snow White, but I drifted. There are no good girls gone wrong, just bad girls found out. When women go wrong, men go right after them. I feel like a million tonight—but one at a time. I've been in more laps than a napkin. A hard man is good to find. Give a man a free hand and he'll run it all over you. I'll try anything once, twice if I like it, three times to make sure.

Ten men waiting for me at the door? Send one of them home, I'm tired. It's not the men in my life that count—it's the life in my men. Is that a gun in your pocket, or are you just glad to see me?

Mae West

With her salacious glances and innuendo-laden retorts, Mae West was once Hollywood's most popular vamp. Raised on the stages of vaudeville, West wooed audiences with her sultry style and revealing costumes. Much more than just a sex symbol, she authored many provocative plays that often drew the ire of censors. Discouraged by the conservative attitudes of New York, West took her talents to Hollywood in the early thirties and starred in numerous movies. Despite her sexy reputation, West was a clean-living woman who didn't drink or smoke, but professionally she was one of the sassiest, smart-mouthed sirens of all time.

It's better to be looked over than overlooked.
I'm single because I was born that way.
One and one is two, and two and two is four, and five will get you ten if you know how to work it.
So many men, so little time.
When I'm good, I'm very, very good. When I'm bad, I'm better.

There was a young
lady of Norway
Swung on a trapeze
in a doorway.
With her legs opened wide,
To her lover she cried,
"I think I've discovered
one more way."

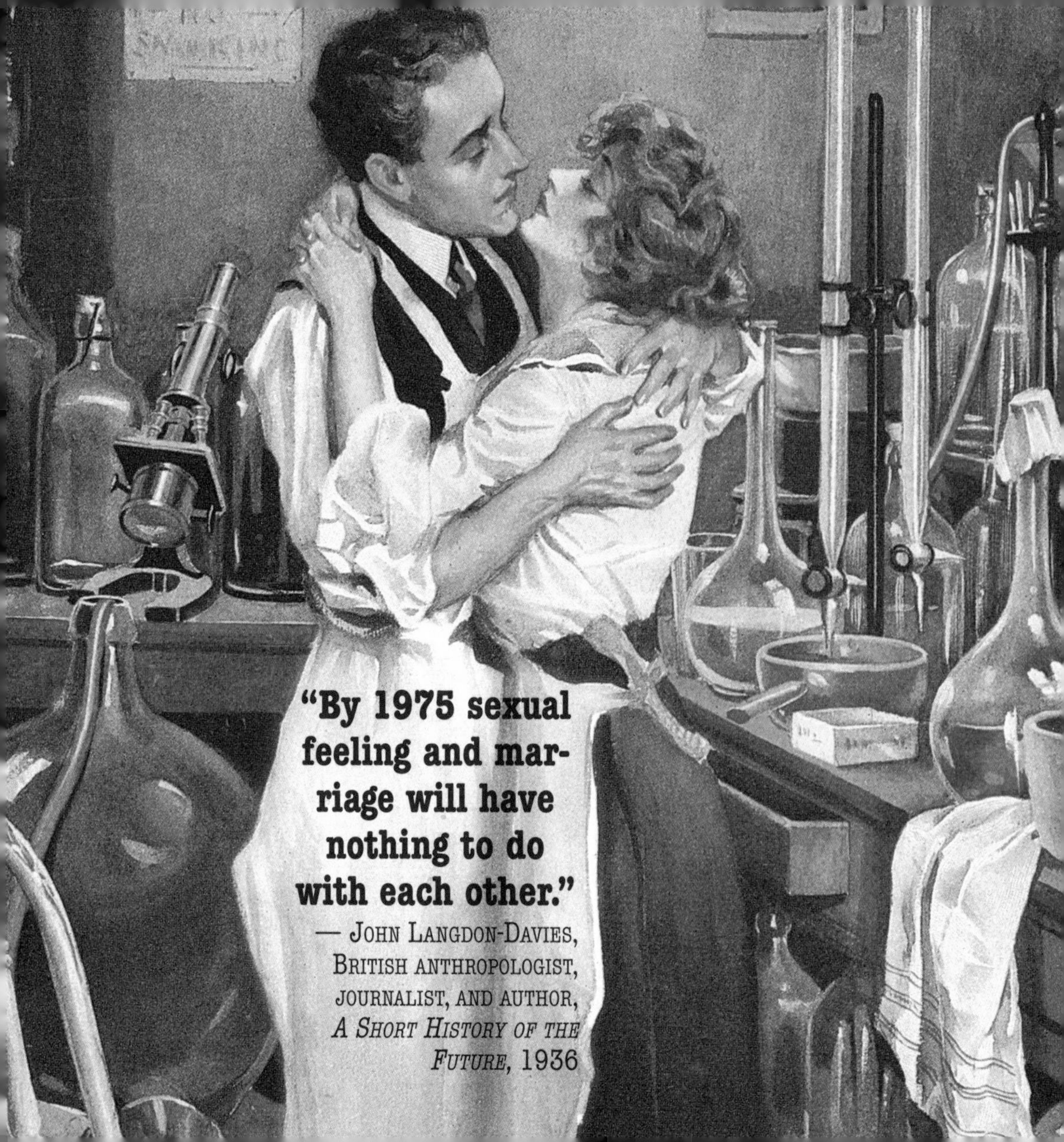
"By 1975 sexual feeling and marriage will have nothing to do with each other."
— JOHN LANGDON-DAVIES, BRITISH ANTHROPOLOGIST, JOURNALIST, AND AUTHOR, *A SHORT HISTORY OF THE FUTURE*, 1936

REAL Funny

EATING CROW: SCIENCE & TECHNOLOGY

Actual statements and comments made by various people throughout history

"Everything that can be invented has been invented."
— Charles H. Duell, Commissioner, U.S. Office of Patents, 1899

"It's a scientific fact that if you shave your mustache, you weaken your eyes."
— William Murray, Governor of Oklahoma, 1932

"The energy produced by the atom is a very poor kind of thing. Anyone who expects a source of power from the transformation of these atoms is talking moonshine."
— Lord Ernest Rutherford, president of Experimental Physics at Cambridge University, after splitting the atom for the first time, September, 1933

"[Man will never reach the moon] regardless of all future scientific advances."
— Dr. Lee DeForest, inventor of the audion tube, *The New York Times*, February 25, 1957

"I think there is a world market for maybe five computers."
— Thomas Watson, chairman of IBM, 1943

"[By 1940] the relativity theory will be considered a joke."
— George Francis Gilette, American engineer and writer, 1929

"There is no reason anyone would want a computer in their home."
— Ken Olson, president, chairman and founder of Digital Equipment Corp., 1977

"The wireless music box has no imaginable commercial value. Who would pay for a message sent to nobody in particular?"
— David Sarnoff's associates in response to his urgings for investment in the radio in the 1920s

"What can be more palpably absurd than the prospect held out of locomotives traveling twice as fast as stagecoaches?"
— *The Quarterly Review*, England, March, 1825

"The concept is interesting and well-formed, but in order to earn better than a 'C,' the idea must be feasible."

—A Yale University management professor in response to Fred Smith's paper proposing reliable overnight delivery service. Smith went on to found Federal Express Corp.

"Television won't matter in your lifetime or mine."

— Rex Lambert, editorial in *The Listener*, 1936

"Computers in the future may weigh no more than 1.5 tons."

—*Popular Mechanics*, forecasting the relentless march of science, 1949

"Make no mistake, this weapon will change absolutely nothing."

— French Director-General of Infantry, dismissing the importance of the machine gun in warfare to the members of the French parliament, 1910

"But what ... is it good for?"

—Engineer at the Advanced Computing Systems Division of IBM, 1968, commenting on the microchip

"The horse is here to stay, but the automobile is only a novelty—a fad."

— President of the Michigan Savings Bank, advising Henry Ford's lawyer not to invest in the Ford Motor Company, 1903

"God himself could not sink this ship."

— Titanic deckhand, Southampton, England, April 10, 1912

"This 'telephone' has too many shortcomings to be seriously considered as a means of communication. The device is inherently of no value to us."

—Western Union internal memo, 1876

"I have traveled the length and breadth of this country and talked with the best people, and I can assure you that data processing is a fad that won't last out the year."

—The editor in charge of business books for Prentice Hall, 1957

"Drill for oil? You mean drill into the ground to try and find oil? You're crazy."

—Drillers who Edwin L. Drake tried to enlist to his project to drill for oil in 1859

"Heavier-than-air flying machines are impossible."
—Lord Kelvin, president, Royal Society, 1895

For answers see bottom of page 113.

1. How many letters are in the alphabet?

2. There is a common English word that is nine letters long. Each time you remove a letter from it, it still remains an English word—from nine letters right down to a single letter. What is the original word, and what are the words that it becomes after removing one letter at a time?

3. The word CANDY can be spelled using just two letters. Can you figure out how?

4. What are the next three letters in this riddle?

O T T F F S S _ _ _

5. What is the word that leaves some left over even when you take away the whole?

6. What six-letter word in the English language contains ten other words without rearranging any of its letters?

7. Why is the letter D like a sailor?

8. Name an English word of more than four letters that both begins and ends with the letters "he" in that order. There are two possible answers. "Hehe" is not acceptable. Haha!

9. What is the next letter in the series "B, C, D, E, G, ___"? Why?

10. What expression is depicted in these letters: GR12"AVE

11. What Spanish instrument's familiar name and fisherman's occupation are the same?

12. What English word has three consecutive double letters?

13. We're five little items of an everyday sort, you'll find us all in "A Tennis Court." What are we?

Riddles: Letters & Words

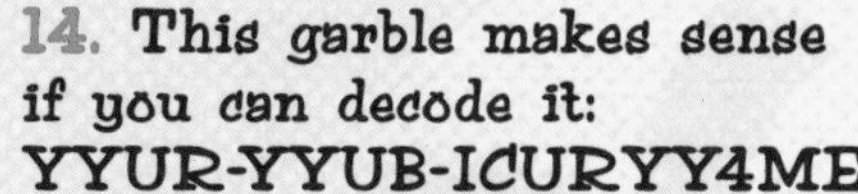

14. This garble makes sense if you can decode it:
YYUR-YYUB-ICURYY4ME

15. What state is round at both ends and high in the middle?

16. If you cross out all unnecessary letters in the following string of letters, a logical sentence will remain. Can you see it?

AALLLOUGNINCEACELSSSEANRYTELNETCTEERS

17. This is an unusual paragraph. I'm curious how quickly you can find out what is so unusual about it. It looks so plain you would think nothing was wrong with it! In fact, nothing is wrong with it! It is unusual though. Study it, and think about it, but you still may not find anything odd. But if you work at it a bit, you might find out! Try to do so without any coaching!

Answers: **1.** 11. T-H-E-A-L-P-H-A-B-E-T. **2.** The base word is Startling - starting - staring - string - sting - sing - sin - in - I. **3.** C and Y. **4.** E N T. They represent the first letter when writing the numbers one thru ten. **5.** The word "Wholesome." **6.** The word is "Spared." The ten words are: ***spa, spar, spare, pa, par, pare, pared, are, re,*** and ***red***. **7.** It follows the C (sea). **8.** "Headache" or "Heartache." **9.** The next letter would be "P." They all rhyme. **10.** One foot in the grave! **11.** Castanet (cast a net). **12.** Bookkeeper. **13.** The five vowels: A E I O U. **14.** Too wise you are, too wise you be, I see you are too wise for me. Spoken as: 2YY's U R - 2YY's U B - I C U R 2YY's 4 ME! **15.** OHIO. **16.** If you cross out the letters in "ALL UNNECESSARY LETTERS," then the remaining letters will spell "A LOGICAL SENTENCE". **17.** The letter "e," which is the most common letter in the English language, does not appear once in the long paragraph.

Dear Sir

pranks & gags

INVISIBLE INK

Want to send a secret message that only the recipient should see? Follow these easy directions to make invisible ink and use it to write a top-secret letter or create invisible invitations for an April Fools' Day party. Just be sure to include a note on how to decode the message, or else you'll be hosting a party for one.

Ingredients: lemons or lemon juice, toothpick, paintbrush, cotton swab (or similar implement), paper, heat source (lightbulb or iron)

For your eyes only!

1. Squeeze lemons and collect their juice in a small bowl. Bottled lemon juice works just as well.
2. Dip a cotton swab or toothpick into the lemon juice and write your secret message on a piece of white paper.
3. Allow the paper to dry completely, preferably overnight.
4. To read your invisible message, hold the paper up to a lightbulb or use an iron to warm the sheet. Be careful not to burn the paper!
5. The heat will cause the lemon juice to darken to a pale brown, revealing your heretofore invisible message.

Milk, white wine, onion juice, orange juice, and vinegar also work well as invisible inks. These organic compounds burn at a different temperature than paper when heated, causing the invisible message to turn brown.

Advice on Writing

The following tips may be helpful for all you would-be or actual writers out there.

1. Avoid alliteration. Always.
2. Prepositions are not words to end sentences with.
3. Avoid clichés like the plague (They are old hat).
4. Parenthetical remarks (however relevant) are unnecessary.
5. Contractions aren't necessary.
6. Foreign words and phrases are not apropos.
7. One should never generalize.
8. Comparisons are as bad as clichés.
9. Don't be redundant; don't use more words than necessary; it's highly superfluous.
10. Be more or less specific.
11. One-word sentences? Eliminate.
12. Analogies in writing are like feathers on a snake.
13. Go around the barn at high noon to avoid colloquialisms.
14. Even if a mixed metaphor sings, it should be derailed.
15. Who needs rhetorical questions?
16. Exaggeration is a billion times worse than understatement.
17. And, don't plagiarize (with a nod to Holcomb B. Noble and the *NY Times*).

A Letter from E. B. White to the ASPCA

E. B. White penned the following letter to the ASPCA in response to receiving a notice that his dog, Minnie, was illegally unlicensed.

12 April 1951
The American Society for the Prevention of Cruelty to Animals
York Avenue and East 92nd Street
New York, 28, NY

Dear Sirs:
I have your letter, undated, saying that I am harboring an unlicensed dog in violation of the law. If by "harboring" you mean getting up two or three times every night to pull Minnie's blanket up over her, I am harboring a dog all right. The blanket keeps slipping off. I suppose you are wondering by now why I don't get her a sweater instead. That's a joke on you. She has a knitted sweater, but she doesn't like to wear it for sleeping; her legs are so short they work out of a sweater and her toenails get caught in the mesh, and this disturbs her rest. If Minnie doesn't get her rest, she feels it right away. I do myself, and of course with this night duty of mine, the way the blanket slips and all, I haven't had any real rest in years. Minnie is twelve.

In spite of what your inspector reported, she has a license. She is licensed in the state of Maine as an unspayed bitch, or what is more commonly called an "unspaded" bitch. She wears her metal license tag but I must say I don't particularly care for it, as it is in the shape of a hydrant, which seems to me a feeble gag, besides being pointless in the case of a female. It is hard to believe that any state in the Union would circulate a gag like that and make people pay money for it, but Maine is always thinking of something. Maine puts up roadside crosses along the highways to mark the spots where people have lost their lives in motor accidents, so the highways are beginning to take on the appearance of a cemetery, and motoring in Maine has become a solemn experience, when one thinks mostly about death. I was driving along a road near Kittery the other day thinking about death and all of a sudden I heard the spring peepers. That changed me right away and I suddenly thought about life. It was the nicest feeling.

You asked about Minnie's name, sex, breed, and phone number. She doesn't answer the phone. She is a dachshund and can't reach it, but she wouldn't answer it even if she could, as she has no interest in outside calls. I did have a dachshund once, a male, who was interested in the telephone, and who got a great many calls, but Fred was an exceptional dog (his name was Fred) and I can't think of anything offhand that he wasn't interested in. The telephone was only one of a thousand things. He loved life—that is, he loved life if by "life" you mean "trouble," and of course the phone is almost synonymous with trouble. Minnie loves life, too, but her idea of life is a warm bed, preferably with an electric pad, and a friend in bed with her, and plenty of shut-eye, night and days. She's almost twelve. I guess I've already mentioned that. I got her from Dr. Clarence Little in 1939. He was using dachshunds in his cancer-research experiments (that was before Winchell was running the thing) and he had a couple of extra puppies, so I wheedled Minnie out of him. She later had puppies by her own father, at Dr. Little's request. What do you think about that for scandal? I know what Fred thought about it. He was some put out.

Sincerely yours,
E. B. White

IF Author Unknown (From *Ann Landers*, March 21, 1999)

If you can start the day without caffeine,
If you can get going without pep pills,
If you can always be cheerful and ignore aches and pains,
If you can resist complaining and boring people with
your troubles,
If you can eat the same food every day and be grateful for it,
If you can understand when your loved ones are too
busy to give you any time,
If you can overlook it when those you love take it out on you
when, through no fault of yours, something goes wrong,
If you can take criticism and blame without resentment,

If you can ignore a friend's limited education
and never correct him,
If you can resist treating a rich friend better
than a poor friend,
If you can face the world without lies and deceit,
If you can conquer tension without medical help,
If you can relax without liquor,
If you can sleep without the aid of drugs,
If you can say honestly that deep in your heart you have
no prejudice against creed, color, religion or politics,
Then, my friend, you are the family dog.

REAL Funny

READ THE SIGNS

Actual signs found in America

ON A DRY CLEANERS IN NEW MEXICO:
"Thirty-eight years on the same spot."

ON A MEDICAL BUILDING IN NEW YORK:
"Mental Health Prevention Center"

ON A CONVALESCENT HOME IN NEW YORK:
"For the sick and tired of the Episcopal church."

ON THE WALLS OF A BALTIMORE ESTATE:
"Trespassers will be prosecuted to the full extent of the law. —Sisters of Mercy"

OUTSIDE A COUNTRY SHOP IN NEW ENGLAND:
"We buy junk and sell antiques."

IN A NEW ENGLAND CHURCH:
"Will the last person to leave please see that the perpetual light is extinguished."

ON A HIGHWAY IN TENNESSEE:
"Take notice: when this sign is under water, this road is impassable."

ON A SHOP'S WALL IN MAINE:
"Our motto is to give our customers the lowest possible prices and workmanship."

IN THE WINDOW OF A GENERAL STORE IN OREGON:
"Why go elsewhere to be cheated, when you can come here?"

IN FRONT OF A CAR WASH IN NEW HAMPSHIRE:
"If you can't read this, it's time you wash your car."

ON A POSTER ON A TELEPHONE POLE IN OREGON:
"Are you an adult that cannot read? If so, we can help."

ON A DRY CLEANING STORE IN PENNSYLVANIA:
"Drop your pants here and you will receive prompt attention."

ON AN OUTSIDE SIGN AT A SUMMER CAMP:
"In case of flood, proceed uphill. In case of flash flood, proceed uphill quickly."

IN A HOTEL ROOM:
"You are invited to take advantage of the chambermaid."

On a Maternity Room door:
"Push, push, push."

In a loan company office:
"Ask about our plans for owning your home."

On a sign in Las Vegas:
"Seeking a sign from God? THIS IS IT!"

On a radiator repair garage:
"Best place to take a leak."

On a bus stop:
"No stopping or standing."

On the wall of a delicatessen:
"Our best is none too good."

On a maternity clothes shop:
"We are open on labor day"

On a roadside truck stop & fuel station sign in Indiana:
"Eat Here and Get Gas."

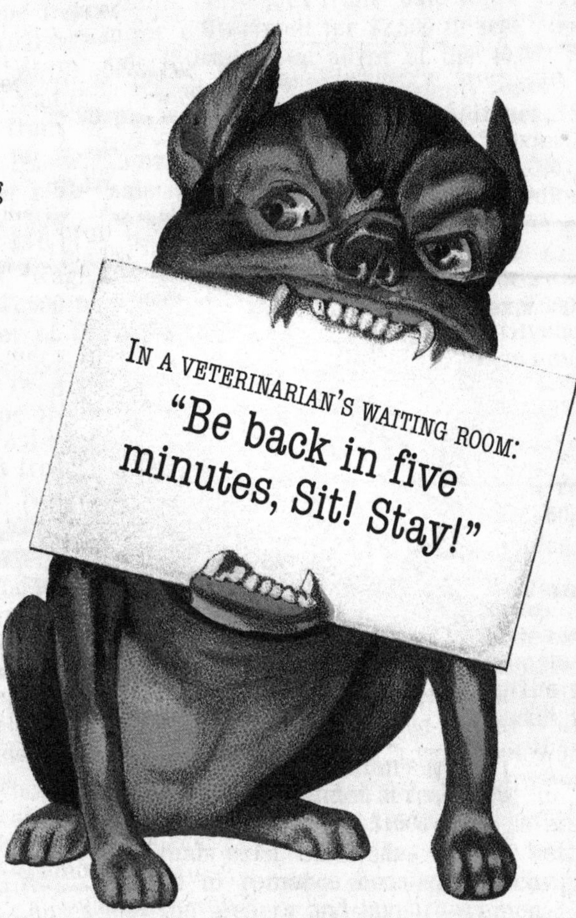

Classic Comics

Frisbeetarianism is the belief that when you die, your soul goes up on the roof and gets stuck. **If it's true that we are here to help others, then what exactly are the others here for?** I was thinking about why people seem to read the Bible a whole lot more as they get older, then it dawned on me… they're cramming for their final exam. **I'm always relieved when someone is delivering a eulogy and I realize I'm listening to it.** Never let the brain idle. "An idle mind is the devil's workshop." And the devil's name is Alzheimer's. **Why is the man (or woman) who invests all your money called a broker?** Why do croutons come in airtight packages? It's just stale bread to begin with. **Why do they sterilize needles for lethal injections?** Why do you press harder on a remote-control when you know the battery is dead? **Some see the glass as half-empty, some see the glass as half-full. I see the glass as too big.** I have as much authority as the Pope, I just don't have as many people who believe it.

George Carlin

For nearly four decades, comedian and social satirist George Carlin has brought his comedy of nonconformity from the fringes to the masses. From his breakthrough role as the hippy-dippy-weatherman on Laugh-In *to his acerbic stand-up routines on the disappointing state of mankind, Carlin's razor-sharp humor remains timeless. With more than twenty albums, two books, and countless live shows under his belt, this classic comedian shows no signs of slowing down.*

Ever notice when you're driving that anyone going slower than you is an idiot, but anyone going faster is a maniac?

If the shoe fits, get another one just like it. **The reason they call it the American Dream is because you have to be asleep to believe it.** I don't own a camera, so I travel with a police sketch artist. **As a matter of principle I never attend the first annual anything.** You rarely meet a wino with perfect pitch. **No one can ever know for sure what a deserted area looks like.** I'd hate to be an alcoholic with Alzheimer's. Imagine needing a drink and forgetting where you put it. **My back hurts; I think I over-schlepped.** Meow means "woof" in cat.

Laughable Limericks

There was a young lady of Niger,
Who smiled as she rode on a tiger.
They returned from the ride
With the lady inside—
And the smile on the face of the tiger!

—Cosmo Monkhouse

There was a young hunter named Shepherd
Who was eaten for lunch by a leopard.
Said the leopard, "Egad!
You'd be tastier, lad,
If you had only been salted and peppered."

A retired Civil Servant from Gateley,
Who lived in a home known as stately,
Kept lions, for fun,
In a wire netting run,
But he hasn't been seen around lately.

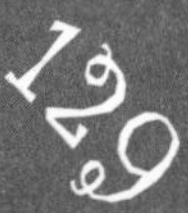

Two backpackers are hiking through the woods when they see a bear about to charge them. One backpacker quickly takes off his hiking boots and changes into running sneakers.

"Are you crazy?" exclaims the other man. "You can't outrun a grizzly!"

"I know," says the man as he finishes tying his sneakers, "but all I have to do is outrun you!"

One day an elephant is walking through the jungle when he comes across a naked man standing in a clearing.

The elephant slowly looks the man up and down and says, "How the hell do ya feed yourself with that?"

Two tall trees are growing in the woods. A small tree begins to grow between them. One tree says to the other, "Is that a son of a beech or a son of a birch?"

The other says he cannot tell. Just then a woodpecker lands on the sapling. One of the tall trees says, "Woodpecker, you are a tree expert. Can you tell if that is a son of a beech or a son of a birch?"

The woodpecker takes a taste of the small tree. He replies, "It is neither a son of a beech nor a son of a birch. That, my friends, is the best piece of ash I have ever had."

Two dogs are barking at each other.

One says, "You're crazy. You should go see a psychiatrist!"

The other replies, "I'd love to, but I'm not allowed on the couch!"

A dog saw somebody putting money into a parking meter and reported to the other dogs, "Hey! They're putting in pay toilets!"

Three handsome male dogs are walking down the street when they see a beautiful female poodle. The males are speechless before her beauty, slobbering on themselves and hoping for just a glance from her in their direction.

Aware of her ogling suitors, the poodle decides to be kind and tells them, "The first one who can use the words "liver" and "cheese" together in an imaginative, intelligent sentence can go out with me."

The sturdy, muscular black lab speaks up quickly and says, "I love liver and cheese."

"Oh, how childish," says the poodle. "That shows no imagination or intelligence whatsoever."

The golden retriever blurts out, "Um. I HATE liver and cheese."

"My, my," said the poodle. "I guess it's hopeless. That's just as dumb as the lab's sentence."

She then turns to the last of the three dogs and says, "How about you, little guy?"

The last of the three, tiny in stature, but big in fame and finesse is the Taco Bell Chihuahua. He gives her a smile and a sly wink, turns to the golden retriever and the lab and says, "Liver alone. Cheese all mine."

The Best Hoaxes *in History*

When it comes to the world of pranks, bigger is definitely better. Freaking out your boss with a fake coffee spill is small beans compared to convincing thousands of Americans that aliens have landed on Earth. We've put together a list of some great pranks and hoaxes throughout history, all of which succeeded in reaching the masses. Warning: Do not try any of these at home!

Ahem . . . Don't Disturb the Squirrels! If you are a speedy runner, better stay out of Cologne. In 1993, a German radio station announced that the city officials had just passed a new law requiring joggers in the park to pace themselves at 6 mph… so as not to overly disturb the squirrels during their mating season. One small "stride" for animal rights!

The Swiss Spaghetti Harvest Time to go spaghetti picking! Satirizing the insular quality of British society at the time, the BBC news show *Panorama* announced in 1957 that thanks to a mild winter and the virtual eradication of the dreaded "spaghetti weevil" there would be a bumper crop of spaghetti in Switzerland this year. Footage of peasants gathering spaghetti out of trees accompanied the story, and many people called the station to see where they could get their own spaghetti trees. Callers were diplomatically told to "place a sprig of spaghetti in a tin of tomato sauce and hope for the best."

War of the Worlds Don't believe your ears! On October 30, 1938, Orson Welles and members of his Mercury Theater Company performed a news-broadcast adaptation of H. G. Wells' *War of the Worlds* on their CBS radio show. Realistically reporting that aliens from Mars were invading New Jersey, Welles' broadcast fooled thousands of listeners when they heard him announce, "Good heavens, something's wiggling out of the shadow like a gray snake. I can see the thing's body now. It's large, large as a bear. It glistens like wet leather." Even Welles was surprised by the size of the frenzied reaction.

Truly Enlightened Pitcher Finally some good news for Mets fans—or so they thought. An article in *Sports Illustrated*'s April 1985 issue lauded the amazing pitching talents of Sidd Finch, supposedly the Mets' new rookie pitcher. Reportedly throwing the ball at 168 mph with spot-on accuracy, Sidd had never played the game before, but instead honed his skills at a Tibetan monastery with "the great poet-saint

Lama Milaraspa." *Sports Illustrated* was inundated with requests for more information, but the new phenom existed only in the mind of the author, George Plimpton.

"UFO" Lands in London Looks like another British invasion! A glowing spacecraft descended over the outskirts of London on March 31, 1989, holding up traffic and terrifying thousands of motorists. When the craft finally landed in a field outside London, locals immediately called the police to warn of an alien invasion. When the police approached the spaceship, a silver-suited figure emerged… and turned out to be Richard Branson, the thirty-six-year-old prank-loving chairman of Virgin Records. The ballooning enthusiast had a balloon built especially to look like a spaceship and was planning to land in London's Hyde Park on April 1st, but was blown off course by the wind and forced to land a day early.

Feelin' Groovy In 1976, Patrick Moore, a British astronomer, announced on BBC Radio 2 that at 9:47 A.M., Pluto would pass behind Jupiter, causing a temporary disturbance in Earth's gravity. He stated that if listeners jumped in the air at the very moment of this occurrence, that they would experience a strange floating sensation. Minutes after 9:47, the station was flooded with calls by people saying they had experienced the sensation, with one woman calling to say that she and her eleven friends had floated around the room!

Arm the Homeless! Here's one way to give to charity. In 1999 the *Phoenix New Times* reprised a prank by hailing the creation of a new charity to benefit the homeless… only instead of food and shelter they would be given guns and ammunition! The charity was to be called the "Arm the Homeless Coalition," and the faux story was even given coverage by *60 Minutes* and the Associated Press before anyone realized the joke.

The Left-Handed Whopper Are you a lefty who always feels left out? This hoax was just for you! In 1998, Burger King took out a full-page advertisement in *USA Today* announcing their new menu item, the

"Left-Handed Whopper" specially designed for the 32 million left-handed Americans. The condiments on this whopper were the same as the regular Whopper, just rotated 180° for the benefit of their lefty customers. This hoax bamboozled many a customer, and spawned demand for a new "Right-Handed Whopper" as well.

Science Bowls a Strike!
Proton, neutron, electron . . . bigon? The science community was "stunned" to read in *Discover* magazine that scientists had actually discovered a new particle of matter. It was coaxed into existence for just a few millionths of a second, but when it materialized it was the size of a bowling ball! Physicist Albert Manque supposedly videotaped it hovering above his computer milliseconds before it exploded. He theorized that the bigon may be responsible for a whole host of mysterious phenomena: sinking soufflés, ball lightning, and spontaneous human combustion.

FatSox You've tried Atkins, the Zone, the Stairmaster, and even the grapefruit diet—so how about trying FatSox? This prank product claimed to suck the fat out of your body through your sweating feet! In 2000, they announced that Esporta Health Clubs created these socks that promised to "banish fat forever!" Invented by Professor Frank Ellis Elgood, they contained a patented polymer, FloraAstraTetrazine, which captured the "excess lipid from the body through sweat." Simply wash the socks after wearing and wash your fat goodbye! Ah, if only it were so easy…

Smellovision In 1965, BBC-TV aired an interview with a professor who claimed to have invented "smellovision," which would allow you to do just that—bring all the aromas produced in the studio into your home. He "demonstrated" his invention by brewing coffee and cutting onions, and many viewers called into say that they could distinctly smell the foods. Talk about the power of suggestion!

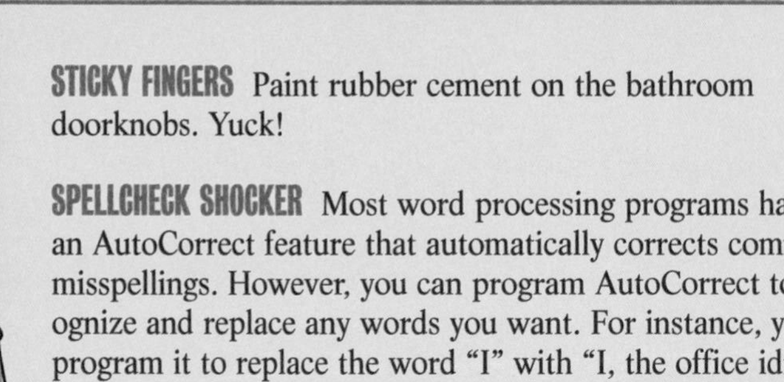

STICKY FINGERS Paint rubber cement on the bathroom doorknobs. Yuck!

SPELLCHECK SHOCKER Most word processing programs have an AutoCorrect feature that automatically corrects common misspellings. However, you can program AutoCorrect to recognize and replace any words you want. For instance, you can program it to replace the word "I" with "I, the office idiot." For a great gag, try this on a coworker's computer. Use your imagination, the possibilities are endless!

TALKING MONITOR If you sit in close proximity to someone at work, plug your keyboard into her computer and when she starts to work type something completely inane or disturbing like, "Alice, you're pressing too hard on my keys today. Did you have another bad weekend?"

RING AROUND THE EAR Coat the receiver of someone's phone with shoe polish and then give them a call. Instant gratification! Make sure you match the colors of the polish and the phone. Small amounts of shaving cream work too.

SAY CHEESE Replace all the pictures on someone's desk with coworkers posed exactly like the replaced images—i.e., everyone from the mail room posed as the victim's family members or the IT guy as her son in his kindergarten graduation robe or, better yet, her daughter in her school uniform.

RINGING WRONGLY Using clear Scotch tape, tape down the rocker on someone's phone so that when it is lifted it keeps on ringing.

CLAP ON/CLAP OFF Ever wonder what to do with that Clapper you got for Christmas? Try plugging it into a coworker's monitor, then clap every time you walk by.

COMPUTER CRASH Close all open files on your fellow cubicle-dweller's computer. Use any appropriate program to create a message saying "***HARD DISK DESTROYED!!!*** and leave it up on the screen. Next, unplug the keyboard so that when your hapless quarry returns you can watch him desperately struggle to make something work. Even when he reboots, the cursor will not move!

CONFETTI MESS Fill a shoe box with confetti. Cover the top with a stiff piece of cardboard that is larger than the box. Holding the cardboard firmly against the box, flip the box over and place it on your victim's desk (or another commonly used surface.) Carefully slide out the piece of cardboard. When your victim picks up the box, the confetti will spill out from underneath and make a very merry mess!

Ah… so many pedestrians, so little time… I know there's a cure for all this bio-terrorism that they send at us, I know there's one and… it lies within Keith Richards. We had gay burglars the other night. They broke in and rearranged the furniture. In California, we have a different kind of police. You get pulled over in West Hollywood, "Stop! Those shoes don't go with those pants." Now in England if you commit a crime, the police don't have a gun and you don't have a gun so if you commit a crime it's "Stop, or I'll say stop again!" My God. We've had cloning in the South for years. Its called cousins. When you look at Prince Charles, don't you think that someone in the Royal family knew someone in the Royal family? If it's the Psychic Network, why do they need a phone number? Cocaine is God's way of saying you're making too much money.

Robin Williams

Acting, stand-up comedy, producing—Robin Williams has done it all. A brilliant performer known for his wild comic style, Williams got his start performing stand-up in nightclubs and landed his breakthrough television role as the alien Mork in a bit part on Happy Days. *He starred in the spin-off* Mork and Mindy *and gained notoriety both on and off the set as an improvisational comedic actor. Williams has had a prolific movie career, earning an Oscar for Best Supporting Actor in* Good Will Hunting. *Esteemed for his brilliant timing, tireless impersonations, and complex dramatic performances, Robin Williams will be entertaining audiences for years to come.*

Classic Comics

Ah yes, divorce, from the Latin word meaning to rip out a man's genitals through his wallet. Shakespeare said, "Kill all the lawyers." That was before there were agents. When my son was born I had this dream that one day he might grow up to be a Nobel Prize winner. But I also had another dream that he might grow up and have to say, "Do you want fries with that?" We're a trillion dollars in debt. Who do we owe this money to? Someone named Vinnie?

Never pick a fight with an ugly person, they've got nothing to lose.

REAL Funny

POLITICAL MISSPEAK

Real statements made by politicians and government officials around the world

"And now, will y'all stand and be recognized?"

— Gib Lewis, Texas Speaker of the House, to a group of people in wheelchairs on Disability Day

"No one wants to say the sky is falling, but in this instance I am afraid the emperor has no clothes. Despite Herculean efforts by the Council and Council staff, we are still only dealing with the tip of the iceberg."

— Charles Millard, NYC councilman, in a press release

"All you have to do is go down to the bottom of your swimming pool and hold your breath."

— David Miller, US DOE spokesperson, on how to protect yourself from nuclear radiation

"It is wonderful to be here in the great state of Chicago."

— Dan Quayle, US vice president

"There are lots more people in the House. I don't know exactly—I've never counted, but at least a couple hundred."

— Dan Quayle, US vice president, on the difference between the House and Senate

"I love California, I practically grew up in Phoenix."

— Dan Quayle, US vice president

"I was recently on a tour of Latin America, and the only regret I have was that I didn't study Latin harder in school so I could converse with those people."

— Dan Quayle, US vice president

"Republicans have been accused of abandoning the poor. It's the other way around. They never vote for us."

— Dan Quayle, US vice president

"You mean there are two Koreas?"

— US ambassador designate to Singapore Richard Kneip, after being asked his opinion during congressional hearings on the North Korea–South Korea conflict.

"You don't tell us how to stage the news, and we don't tell you how to report it."

— LARRY SPEAKES, PRESS SECRETARY FOR PRESIDENT GEORGE BUSH

"We know smoking tobacco is not good for kids, but a lot of other things aren't good. Drinking's not good. Some would say milk's not good."

— BOB DOLE

"I am not a chauvinist, obviously.... I believe in women's rights for every woman but my own."

— CHICAGO MAYOR HAROLD WASHINGTON

"I make my decisions horizontally, not vertically."

— SENATOR BOB KERRY

"We're not without accomplishment. We have managed to distribute poverty equally."

— NGUYEN CO THACH, VIETNAMESE FOREIGN MINISTER

"There is no prostitution in China; however, we do have some women who make love for money."

— CHINESE FOREIGN MINISTRY SPOKESPERSON

"A zebra cannot change its spots."

— US VICE PRESIDENT AL GORE

"I am not wanting to make too long speech tonight as I am knowing your old English saying, 'Early to bed and up with the cock.'"

— HUNGARIAN DIPLOMAT IN A SPEECH TO AN EMBASSY PARTY

"His boss may have needed choking. It may have been justified... someone should have asked the question, 'What prompted that?'"

— San Francisco mayor Willie Brown defending basketball star Latrell Sprewell, who was fired for choking and threatening to kill his coach

"One can't tolerate certain sights. From next summer, there will be no more flab all over the place: buttocks, cellulite thighs, and drooping boobs will all be banished."

— Andrew Guglieri, mayor of Diano Marina, Italy, announcing his hopes to ban certain women from wearing bikinis in town

"The president doesn't want any yes-men and yes-women around him. When he says no, we all say no."

— Elizabeth Dole, then assistant for public liaison to President Reagan, later presidential candidate

"Why can't the Jews and the Arabs just sit down together and settle this like good Christians?"

— An unnamed senator

"In the whole history of the world, whenever a meat-eating race has gone to war against a non-meat-eating race, the meat eaters won. It produces superior people. We have the books of history."

— Senator Carl Curits during a debate on banning DES as a food additive for livestock

"Even if he were mediocre, there are a lot of mediocre judges and people and lawyers. Don't they deserve some representation on the court?"

— Senator Roman Hruska defending Judge Harold Carswell, the first Nixon nominee for the Supreme Court, against charges that he was mediocre

"First, they tax our beer, then they tax cigarettes. Now they are going to increase the tax on gasoline. All that's left are our women."

— Senator John East

"I haven't committed a crime. What I did was fail to comply with the law."

— David Dinkins, New York City mayor, answering accusations that he failed to pay his taxes

"I intend to open this country up to democracy, and anyone who is against that, I will jail, I will crush."
— General João Baptista Figueiredo upon becoming president of Brazil

"Sometimes in order to make progress and move ahead, you have to stand up and do the wrong thing."
— Representative Gary Ackerman explaining why he supported the new welfare bill

"If crime went down one hundred percent, it would still be fifty times higher than it should be."
— Councilman John Bowman commenting on the high crime rate in Washington, DC

"Women are hard enough to handle now without giving them a gun."
— Senator Barry Goldwater talking about women in the armed services

"I can't believe that we are going to let a majority of the people decide what's best for this state."
— Representative John Travis of the Louisiana legislature

"What right does Congress have to go around making laws just because they deem it necessary?"
—Marion Barry, mayor of Washington, DC

"First, it was not a strip bar, it was an erotic club. And second, what can I say? I'm a night owl."
— Marion Barry, mayor of Washington, DC

You might be a Democrat if...

You've named your kids "Stardust" or "Moonbeam."

You've uttered the phrase "There ought to be a law" at least once a week.

You have ever found yourself nodding vigorously and saying, "Someone finally said it right" during an episode of Oprah.

All of your 1970s BEWARE OF GLOBAL FREEZING signs now have BEWARE OF GLOBAL WARMING on the back.

Your friends told you how much fun you had at the Grateful Dead show, but you're not sure what year you saw them.

You know more than two people who have a degree in "Womyn's Studies."

You blame things on "The Man."

You've ever called the meter maid a fascist.

You are giddy at the prospect of the return of bell-bottoms.

You know two or more people with "concrete proof" that the Pentagon is covering up Roswell, the Kennedy assassination, or the CIA's role in creating AIDS.

You've ever owned a VW bug or ridden in a microbus.

You own something that says "Dukakis for President" and still display it.

You object to little old ladies wearing fur but not big, mean bikers wearing leather.

You might be a Republican if…

You've tried to argue that poverty could be abolished if people were allowed to keep more of their minimum wage.

You've ever uttered the phrase, "Why don't we just bomb the sons of bitches?"

You don't let your kids watch *Sesame Street* because you accuse Bert and Ernie of "sexual deviance" or you've ever told a child that Oscar the Grouch "lives in a trash can because he is lazy and doesn't want to contribute to society."

You've ever called a secretary or waitress "honey."

You use any of these terms to describe your wife: "old ball and chain," "little woman," and/or "tax credit."

You think Birkenstock was that radical rock concert in 1969.

You've ever said, "Clean air? Looks clean to me."

You've ever called education a luxury.

You wonder if donations to the Pentagon are tax deductible.

You've ever based an argument on the phrase, "Well, tradition dictates…"

You think all artists are gay.

You've ever urged someone to pull themselves up by their bootstraps, when they don't even have shoes.

There was a young
maid from Madras

Who had a
magnificent ass;

Not rounded
and pink,

As you probably
think—

It was grey,
had long ears,
and ate grass.

Laughable Limericks

There was an old codger of Broome,
Who kept a baboon in his room.
"It reminds me," he said,
"Of a friend who is dead."
But he never would tell us of whom.

There was an old widower, Doyle,
Who wrapped up his wife in tin foil.
He thought it would please her
To stay in the freezer—
And, anyway, outside she'd spoil.

There was a young lady of Venice,
Who used hard-boiled eggs to play tennis.
When they said, "It seems wrong."
She remarked, "Go along!
You don't know how prolific my hen is."

"A fine View."
What's the use?
Ogden Nash
Sure, deck your limbs in pants;
Yours are the limbs, my sweeting.
You look divine as you advance—
Have you seen yourself retreating?

GET OUT!

Chris Rock

How can a brother own two cars and still live with his mamma? Even if you've got one car—get out!

Guys who won't move out are a sad phenomenon. Women sometimes *have* to stay until they're old. It can be kind of cute. But men? Get out! I have 35-year-old friends who still live at home. Get out! There's only one thing worse than a man that old still living with his parents, and that's any woman willing to sneak into his room. Once you get past a certain age, you shouldn't be tiptoeing past anybody.

"Shh, take off your shoes."

Later, they're having sex, and he grunts, "Say my name!"

But before she can say, "Gregory," he cuts her off: "No! Whisper it. I don't want to wake my parents."

I don't visit my friends who won't move out. Do you know how depressing it is to sit in the same room you two sat in when you were both 14? There's the little-ass dresser, the little-ass bed, and the poster of Tony Dorset on the wall.

Get out!

You can always tell when they're not planning to leave because they start doing renovations. "I'ma knock this wall out, put in a fish tank, some mirrors. Did you know mirrors make a room seem bigger?"

Some of them just try to play it off: "But I'm just taking care of moms." Bullshit. You can't take care of yourself. Your mom could make some money renting the room if you got the f**k out.

The saddest ones are the brothers waiting for their parents to die.

"Well, you know this is all gonna be mine."

What? Your mother's only 54. What are you going to do, poison her?

Hard work never killed anybody, but why take the chance?
—EDGAR BERGEN

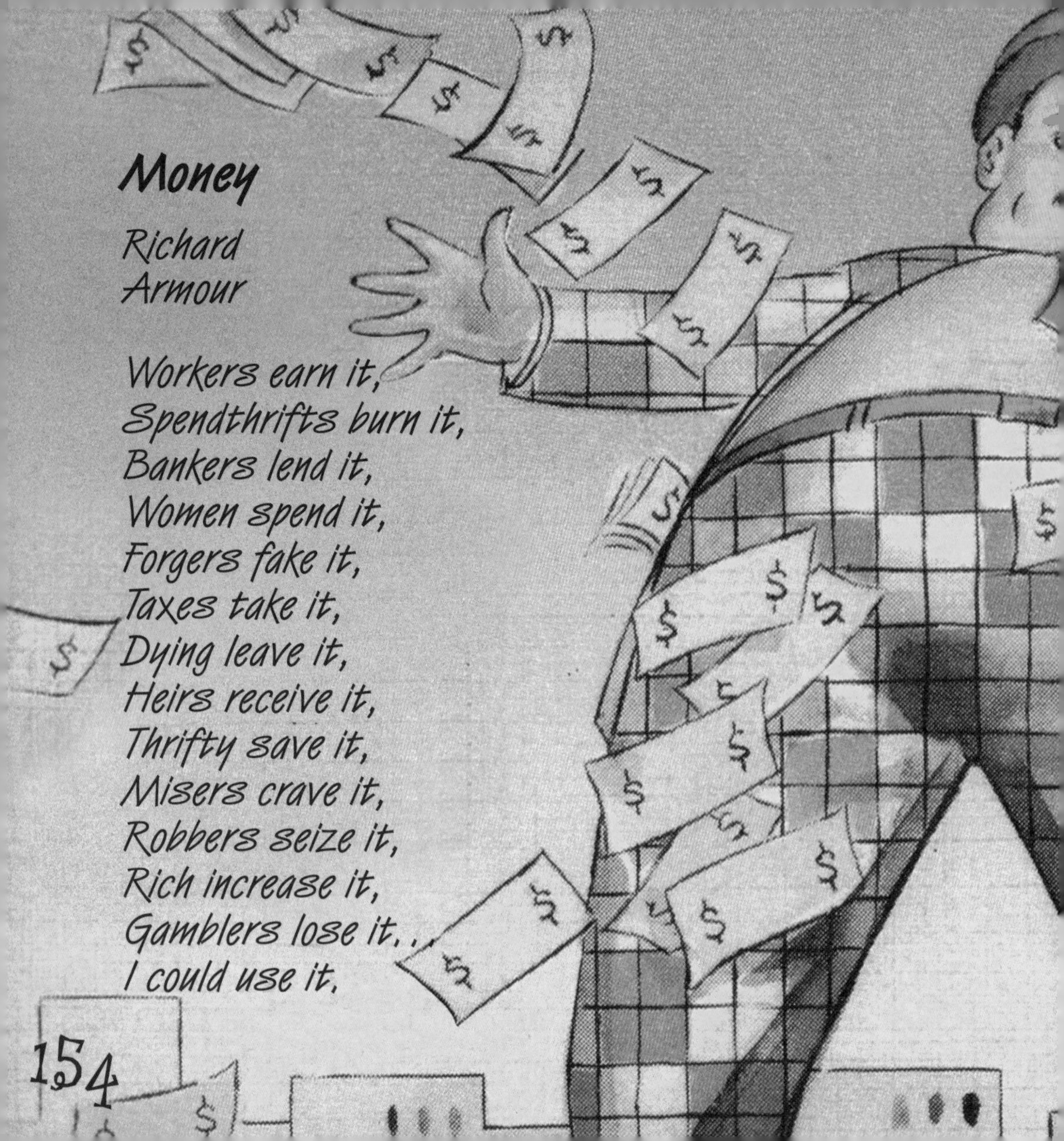

Money

Richard Armour

Workers earn it,
Spendthrifts burn it,
Bankers lend it,
Women spend it,
Forgers fake it,
Taxes take it,
Dying leave it,
Heirs receive it,
Thrifty save it,
Misers crave it,
Robbers seize it,
Rich increase it,
Gamblers lose it...
I could use it.

I was a boring child. Whenever we played doctor, the other children always made me the anesthesiologist. I admire the Pope. I have a lot of respect for anyone who can tour without an album. You know the oxygen masks on airplanes? I don't think there's really any oxygen. I think they're just to muffle the screams. I was a vegetarian until I started leaning toward the sunlight. I wonder if other dogs think poodles are members of a weird religious cult. I hate doing laundry. I don't separate the colors from the whites. I put them together and let them learn from their cultural differences. Whenever I date a guy, I think, "Is this the man I want my children to spend their weekends with?" After you've dated someone it should be legal to stamp them with what's wrong with them so the next person doesn't have to start from scratch. After two years I said to my boyfriend, "Either tell me your

Rita Rudner

This soft-spoken comedienne has parlayed her understated style of humor into a full-blown comic career. She has amused television audiences on Late Night with David Letterman, The Tonight Show, *and in her HBO special* Born To Be Mild, *and performed in comedy clubs around the United States. Her cynical wit, sophisticated delivery, and killer timing set her apart from the crowd and have made her one of the most lovable ladies of comedy.*

Classic Comics

My last credit card bill was so big, before I opened it I actually heard a drum roll.

name or it's over." When I eventually met Mr. Right I had no idea that his first name was Always. I asked my husband if he wanted to be in the room with me when I gave birth. He said, "It would have to be a big room, and there would have to be a bar at one end." My husband is from England and has never seen a football game before. So I could tell him anything I wanted. I told him it was over at halftime. I love being married. It's so great to find that one special person you want to annoy for the rest of your life. In Hollywood a marriage is a success if it outlasts milk. My parents have been married for fifty years. I asked my mother how they did it. She said, "You just close your eyes and pretend it's not happening." Neurotics build castles in the air, psychotics live in them. My mother cleans them. I don't plan to grow old gracefully. I plan to have face-lifts until my ears meet.

REAL Funny

LAUGHABLE LAWS

Actual laws and statutes

Our Furry & Feathered Friends

In Honolulu, Hawaii, it is against the law to annoy a bird in any park.

In Los Angeles, it is illegal to be in possession of a hippopotamus.

In Brooklyn, New York, it is against the law to let a donkey sleep in a bathtub.

In Barber, North Carolina, it is unlawful for cats and dogs to fight.

In Pauling, Ohio, it is legal for a police officer to bite a dog in an attempt to quiet him.

In Tuscumbia, Alabama, it is against the law for more than eight rabbits to live on the same block.

In Los Angeles, California, hunting moths under a streetlight is against the law.

That's Awful Personal!

In Indiana, it is against the law to take a bath during the winter months.

In Brainerd, Minnesota, there is a law requiring every male to grow a beard.

In Nogales, Arizona, it is unlawful to wear suspenders.

In Nebraska, sneezing in public is illegal.

In Massachusetts, snoring is prohibited unless all bedroom windows are closed and securely locked.

Work, Food & Play

In New Jersey, it is illegal to slurp your soup.

In Corvallis, Oregon, young women are forbidden to drink coffee after 6 P.M.

In the District of Columbia, it is illegal to fly a kite.

In Belton, Missouri, it is illegal to have a snowball fight.

In Chicago, it is forbidden to bring a French poodle to the opera.

Love & Marriage

In Dixie, Idaho, a husband can be fined if his wife yells at him in public and a crowd gathers.

In California, the law says a housewife must cook her dustcloth after using it.

In Kentucky, marrying the same man four times is against the law.

In Lebanon, Tennessee, a husband cannot kick his wife out of bed for having cold feet; however, a wife can kick her husband out of bed without any reason.

In Florida, there is a law that forbids a housewife from breaking more than three dishes a day.

In Compton, California, dancing cheek-to-cheek is prohibited.

In Kennesaw, Georgia, every head of household is required to own a firearm.

In Dyersburg, Tennessee, it is illegal for a woman to telephone a man asking for a date.

In Portland, Maine, it is illegal to tickle a girl under the chin with a feather duster.

In Stockton, California, it is illegal to wiggle on the dance floor.

In Hartford, Connecticut, the law says you may never kiss your wife on a Sunday.

In Halethorpe, Maryland, a kiss cannot last longer than a second.

In Cedar Rapids, Iowa, it is illegal to kiss a stranger.

In Iowa, kisses may last for no more than five minutes.

In Iowa, a man with a moustache may never kiss a woman in public.

In Tennessee, it is illegal to drive a car while sleeping.

In Memphis, Tennessee, a woman may not drive a car unless a man runs in front of the car waving a red flag.

Gettin' Around

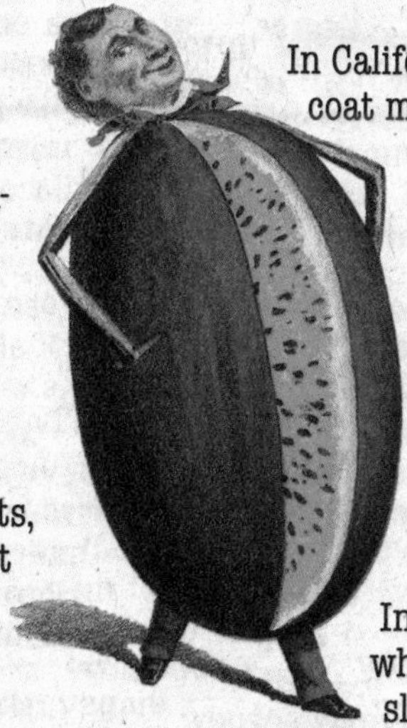

In Johnson City, New York, a person is not allowed to wander from the left side to the right side of the sidewalk.

In Maine, walking with your shoelaces untied is illegal.

In Marblehead, Massachusetts, it is illegal to cross the street on Sunday, unless it is absolutely necessary.

In Thousand Oaks, California, it is against the law to sit on the curb.

In Cambridge, Massachusetts, it is illegal to throw orange peels on the sidewalk.

In California, a woman in a housecoat may not drive a car.

In Hammond, Indiana, it is illegal to throw watermelon seeds on the sidewalk.

In Alabama, driving a car while barefoot or in bedroom slippers is forbidden.

In San Francisco, it's illegal to wipe your car with used underwear.

In Atlanta, Georgia, a law forbids "smelly" people to ride public streetcars.

A young lawyer meets the devil at a bar association convention and the devil says, "Listen, if you give me your soul and the souls of everyone in your family, I'll make you a full partner in your firm."

And the young lawyer says, "So... what's the catch?"

Two divorce lawyers were having drinks in a lounge after a grueling day in the courts. In walked the most stunning woman either of the lawyers had seen in a long time.

One of the lawyers remarked, "Boy! I sure would like to screw her!"

"Out of what?" the other replied.

Lawyer Jokes

Alice walked into a post office one day to see a middle-aged, balding man standing at the counter methodically placing "Love" stamps on bright pink envelopes with hearts all over them. He then took out a perfume bottle and started spraying each envelope. Alice's curiosity getting the better of her, she went up to the man and asked him what he was doing.

The man said, "I'm sending out one thousand Valentines cards signed 'Guess who?'"

"But why?" Alice asked.

"I'm a divorce lawyer," the man replied.

A young boy walked up to his father and asked, "Daddy, does a lawyer ever tell the truth?"

The father thought for a moment. "Yes, son. Sometimes a lawyer will do anything to win a case."

A lawyer sent a note to a client:

"Dear Jim: Thought I saw you on the street the other day. Crossed over to say hello, but it wasn't you, so I went back. One-tenth of an hour: $25."

Lawyer Jokes

A housewife, an accountant, and a lawyer were asked, "How much is two plus two?"

The housewife replied, "Four."

The accountant said, "I think it's either three or four. Let me run these figures through my spreadsheet one more time."

The lawyer pulled the drapes, dimmed the lights, and asked in a hushed voice, "How much do you want it to be?"

Changing lawyers is like moving to a different deck chair on the Titanic.

A man called his lawyer, doctor, and his priest to his deathbed and handed each of them an envelope containing $25,000 in cash. He made them each promise that after he died they would place the three envelopes in his coffin so he would have enough money to enjoy the afterlife.

A week later the man passed away. At the funeral, the lawyer, doctor, and priest each dutifully put an envelope in the coffin. Several months later, the three men gathered for a drink to have a farewell toast to their dearly departed friend. Soon the clergyman, feeling guilty, confesses there was only $10,000 in the envelope he put in the coffin. Believing that money meant nothing in heaven, he sent it to a mission in South Africa where it was gravely needed. He asked the other two men for their forgiveness.

The doctor, moved by the priest's honesty, admitted that he,

Why won't sharks eat lawyers?
—Professional courtesy

What did the lawyer name his daughter? —Sue

too, had kept some of the money to donate to a medical charity. His envelope had had only $8,000 in it.

By this time the lawyer was seething with self-righteous outrage. "I am the only one who kept his promise to our dying friend. I want you both to know that the envelope that I placed in the coffin contained the full amount. Indeed, my envelope contained a personal check for the entire $25,000."

Joan, an investment counselor, decided to open her own firm. Her business flourished and soon she decided she needed to hire an in-house counsel, so she began to interview lawyers.

"As I'm sure you understand," she began with her first applicant, "in a business such as this, our personal integrity must be beyond question." She leaned forward. "Mr. Jackson, are you an honest lawyer?"

"Honest?" replied the job applicant. "Let me tell you something about honest. Why, I'm so honest that my father lent me $15,000 for my education and I paid back every penny right after I tried my very first case."

"Impressive. And what sort of case was that?"

The lawyer squirmed in his seat. "He sued me for the money."

I'm very pleased to be here. Let's face it, at my age I'm very pleased to be anywhere. **You know you're getting old when you stoop to tie your shoelaces and wonder what else you could do while you're down there.** First you forget names, then you forget faces. Next you forget to pull your zipper up and finally, you forget to pull it down. **Old age is when you resent the swimsuit issue of "Sports Illustrated" because there are fewer articles to read.** When I was a boy the Dead Sea was only sick. **People ask me what I'd most appreciate getting for my eighty-seventh birthday. I'll tell you: a paternity suit.** Happiness is a good martini, a good meal, a good cigar and a good woman… or a bad woman, depending on how much happiness you can stand. **It takes only one drink to get me drunk. The**

George Burns

Born into poverty on January 20, 1896 on New York's Lower East Side as Nathan Birnbaum, George Burns lived the ultimate rags-to-riches life. Short on formal education—having quit school in the fourth grade to help with family finances—he had plenty of talent and, more importantly, a relentless drive to be in show biz. His professional career began in vaudeville at the age of seven, but real success eluded him until he met and teamed up with performer (and future wife) Gracie Allen. With George's dry-as-dust wit and brilliant timing and Gracie's kooky, scatter-brained character, Burns and Allen quickly became a hit. They went on to work in movies and radio and starred in their own TV show from 1950–1958. Never one for retirement, George made an astounding comeback at the age of eighty with his Oscar-winning performance in The Sunshine Boys *in 1975. George Burns died March 9, 1996 in Beverly Hills.*

trouble is, I can't remember if it's the thirteenth or the fourteenth. I love to sing, and I love to drink scotch. Most people would rather hear me drink scotch. Happiness is having a large, loving, caring, close-knit family in another city. There are two kinds of cruises—pleasure and with children. Too bad that all the people who know how to run the country are busy driving taxicabs and cutting hair. You've got to be honest; if you can fake that, you've got it made. Retire? I'm going to stay in show business until I'm the only one left.

And God said: Let there be Satan, so people don't blame everything on me. And let there be lawyers, so people don't blame everything on Satan.

Bohemia

Dorothy Parker

Authors and actors and artists and such
Never know nothing, and never know much.
Sculptors and singers and those of their kidney
Tell their affairs from Seattle to Sydney.
Playwrights and poets and such horses' necks
Start off from anywhere, end up at sex.
Diarists, critics, and similar roe
Never say nothing, and never say no.
People Who Do Things exceed my endurance;
God, for a man that solicits insurance!

A frog wanted to buy a new lily pond but had run out of money so he went to the bank for a loan. He sat down at a desk and introduced himself as Kermit Jagger, son of Mick Jagger. He was interviewed by a bank official named Patty Whack who asked the frog what he could offer as collateral. The frog reached into his briefcase and produced a vase but Patty was unimpressed. “I'm afraid we'll need something more than that,” she told the frog. “It's just a cheap knickknack.”

But just to be sure, she decided to show the vase to the bank manager, who knew a lot about antiques. “I've got this frog named Kermit Jagger and he's brought in this vase as collateral. What do you think?”

The manager registered the name, took one look at the vase and said: “It's a knick-knack, Patty Whack, but give the frog a loan. His old man's a Rolling Stone.”

For an Amorous Lady
Theodore Roethke

The pensive gnu, the staid aardvark,
Accept caresses in the dark;
The bear, equipped with paw and snout,
Would rather take than dish it out.
But snakes, both poisonous and garter,
In love are never known to barter;
The worm, though dank, is sensitive:
His noble nature bids him give.

But you, my dearest, have a soul
Encompassing fish, flesh, and fowl.
When amorous arts we would pursue,
You can, with pleasure, bill or coo.
You are, in truth, one in a million,
At once mammalian and reptilian.

classic Comics

I failed to make the chess team because of my height. I believe that sex is a beautiful thing between two people. Between five, it's fantastic. If only God would give me some clear sign! Like making a large deposit in my name at a Swiss bank. Sex between a man and a woman can be wonderful, provided you get between the right man and the right woman. When we played softball, I'd steal second base, feel guilty and go back. And if it turns out that there is a God, I don't believe that he is evil. The worst that can be said is that he's an underachiever. As the poet said, "Only God can make a tree"—probably because it's so hard to figure out how to get the bark on. I can't listen to that much Wagner. I start getting the urge to conquer Poland. I was thrown out of college during my freshman year, for

Woody Allen

Part neurotic New Yorker, part comedian, and part film auteur, Woody Allen is one of the most beloved comic personalities in show business. After getting his start as a television joke writer and stand-up comic, Allen soon moved on to screenwriting and won his first directing credit in 1966 with What's Up, Tiger Lily? *Since then he has written and directed more than thirty films, including* Annie Hall, Manhattan, *and* Hannah and Her Sisters.

Classic Comics

cheating on my metaphysics final. You know, I looked within the soul of the boy sitting next to me. I will not eat oysters. I want my food dead. Not sick—not wounded—dead. I'm astounded by people who want to 'know' the universe when it's so hard to find your way around Chinatown. Love is the answer—but while you're waiting for the answer, sex raises some pretty good questions. Don't knock masturbation, it's sex with someone you love. Sex without love is an empty experience, but as empty experiences go, it's one of the best. What if everything is an illusion and nothing exists? In that case, I definitely overpaid for my carpet. I think crime pays. The hours are good, and you travel a lot. I have an intense desire to return to the womb. Anybody's. You can live to be a hundred if you give up all the things that make you want to live to be a hundred.

Being bisexual doubles your chance of a date on Saturday night.

TO-DAY

The Best Laughs at The Movies

A rainy day, a bowl of popcorn, and a VCR: the perfect ingredients for an afternoon of funny movie magic. Here's a list of some of our favorite comedy rentals, chosen for their timeless appeal and ability to make us laugh as hard the tenth time we see them as we did the first. Will they challenge you intellectually? It's doubtful. Do they have deep social meaning? Probably not. Will they make milk shoot out of your nose? Most definitely.

A Fish Called Wanda (1988) Jamie Lee Curtis and goofy Kevin Kline match half-wits against repressed Brit John Cleese and "animal lover" Michael Palin as they try to recover stolen diamonds.

Abbott and Costello Meet Frankenstein (1948) It's Bud Abbott. Lou Costello. Dracula. The Wolfman. And Frankenstein. What more do you want?

Airplane! (1980) When the crew of an airplane become sick, it's up to ex-pilot Ted Stryker, his wacky ex-girlfriend, an air traffic controller with a major drug problem, and a randy auxiliary pilot to land the plane. Just don't call them Shirley.

Annie Hall (1977) Love in the 1970s never had so many neuroses. Woody Allen and Diane Keaton surf the ups and downs of relationships in this Manhattan love story. See it when your therapist goes out of town.

Arthur (1981) Rampant alcoholism was never so funny! Sloshed millionaire Dudley Moore must clean up his act if he's going to find a way to keep his fortune and win the heart of plebeian Liza Minnelli. John Gielgud is at his acidic best as Arthur's deadpan butler.

Best In Show (2000) Outrageous goings-on at a dog show prove side-splitting, but the real awards go to Fred Willard, an announcer who wouldn't know a Mastiff from a Terrier, and Eugene Levy, a canine-owner with two left feet. Literally.

Blazing Saddles (1974) Mel Brooks skewers old-time Westerns when a decidedly different sheriff comes to save Rock Ridge from the dastardly Hedley Lamar (that's Hed-ley!).

Bringing Up Baby (1938) What do you get when you put a zoologist, an heiress, and a baby leopard together? A major headache and this screwball comedy by Howard Hawks.

Caddyshack (1980) Chevy Chase and Rodney Dangerfield head a cast of lunatics in this slapstick classic about what really goes on at a classy golf course. Don't see it if you plan on eating a Baby Ruth candy bar ever again.

The General (1927) Incredible stunts and fantastic choreography highlight this Civil War story about a lone engineer, played by Buster Keaton, in hot pursuit of his two loves: Annabelle Lee and a locomotive.

Ghostbusters (1984) Proving it takes more than a little ectoplasm to scare off New Yorkers, Bill Murray, Dan Ackroyd, Harold Ramis, and Ernie Hudson battle ghosts, poltergeists, and (most horrifying of all) the Stay-Puft Marshmallow Man.

The Gold Rush (1925) Comic genius Charlie Chaplin gets into mishap after mishap trying to strike gold in Alaska in this comedy classic.

The Jerk (1979) Steve Martin may not know much, but he does know he has a special purpose. Follow the witless wanderings of Navin R. Johnson from his down-South childhood to his success as a tycoon, to his idiotic downfall.

Monty Python and the Holy Grail (1975) Arthur and his knights encounter the Knights Who Say "Ni!", Tim the Enchanter, the Holy Hand Grenade of

Antioch, and a really, really, REALLY vicious rabbit in this truly hilarious send-up by the Monty Python cast.

9 to 5 (1980) Jane Fonda, Dolly Parton, and Lily Tomlin live out the American dream when they kidnap their sexist boss, Dabney Coleman, and hold him hostage. For all those who have had to fetch coffee one too many times.

The Princess Bride (1987) Insecurity and jealousy can break up any relationship. But try dealing with sadistic royalty, some loony miracle workers, a friendly giant, and a horrific fire swamp and see how romantic you feel. Luckily, director Rob Reiner believes in happy endings.

Raising Arizona (1987) You think raising kids is hard? Try stealing one. Nicholas Cage and Holly Hunter get more than they bargained for after kidnapping a baby. One of the best car chase scenes/diaper pickups ever filmed.

Some Like It Hot (1959) Tony Curtis and Jack Lemmon evade 1920s gangsters by heading down to Florida in drag with an all-girl band. Think that sounds complicated? Wait until Marilyn Monroe and her little ukulele enter the picture.

There's Something About Mary (1998) Admit it, how long was it before you put gel in your hair again? Drug-crazed canines, eczema-plagued friends, and one really stuck zipper all try to derail Ben Stiller's quest for love.

This Is Spinal Tap (1984) The mother of all mockumentaries follows metal group Spinal Tap as they struggle (and fail) to finish their careers off with any semblance of dignity. Features the world's loudest amp and a Stonehenge in danger of being crushed by a dwarf.

Tootsie (1982) Desperate-to-work actor Dustin Hoffman learns more about being a man by being a woman on the set of a hilarious soap opera in this classic comedy by Sydney Pollack.

Trading Places (1983) Wisecracking Eddie Murphy teams up with Dan Aykroyd and Jamie Lee Curtis in this 80's satire about declining social mores.

REAL Funny

UNDERAGE ADVICE

Real pearls of wisdom offered by children

"Don't pull dad's finger when he tells you to."

—EMILY, AGE 10

"When your mom is mad at your dad, don't let her brush your hair."

—TAYLIA, AGE 11

"Never hold a dust-buster and a cat at the same time."

—KYOYO, AGE 9

"You can't hide a piece of broccoli in a glass of milk."

—ARMIR, AGE 9

"Stay away from prunes."

—RANDY, AGE 9

"Felt pens are not good to use as lipstick."

—LAUREN, AGE 9

"When you get a bad grade at school, show it to your mom when she's on the phone."

—ALYESHA, AGE 13

"Never try to baptise a cat."

—EILEEN, AGE 8

"When your dad is mad and asks you, 'Do I look stupid?' don't answer him."

—MICHAEL, AGE 14

"Puppies still have bad breath even after eating a Tic Tac."

—ANDREW, AGE 9

"If you want a kitten, start out by asking for a horse."

—NAOMI, AGE 15

"Don't squat with your spurs on."

—NORONHA, AGE 13

"Never trust a dog to watch your food."

—PATRICK, AGE 10

PARENTAL GUIDANCE

Fran Lebowitz

As the title suggests, this piece is intended for those among us who have taken on the job of human reproduction. And while I am not unmindful of the fact that many of my readers are familiar with the act of reproduction only insofar as it applies to a too-recently fabricated Louis XV armoire, I nevertheless feel that certain things cannot be left unsaid. For although distinctly childless myself, I find that I am possessed of some fairly strong opinions on the subject of the rearing of the young. The reasons for this are varied, not to say rococo, and range from genuine concern for the future of mankind to simple, cosmetic disdain.

Being a good deal less villainous than is popularly posed, I do not hold small children entirely accountable for their own behavior. By and large, I feel this burden must be borne by their elders. Therefore, in an effort to make knowledge power, I offer the following suggestions:

Your responsibility as a parent is not as great as you might imagine. You need not supply the world with the next conqueror of disease or major motion-picture star. If your child simply grows up to be someone who does not use the word "collectible" as a noun, you can consider yourself an unqualified success.

Children do not really need money. After all, they don't have to pay rent or send mailgrams. Therefore their allowance should be just large enough to cover chewing gum and an occasional pack of cigarettes.

A child who is not rigorously instructed in the matter of table manners is a child whose future is being dealt with cavalierly. A person who makes an admiral's hat out of a linen napkin is not going to be in wild social demand.

Do not have your child's hair cut by a real hairdresser in a real hairdressing salon. He is, at this point, far too short to be exposed to contempt.

Do not, on a rainy day, ask your child what he feels like doing, because I assure you that what he feels like doing, you won't feel like watching.

Educational television should be absolutely forbidden. It can only lead to unreasonable expectations and eventual disappointment when your child discovers that the letters of the alphabet do not leap up out of books and dance around the room with royal-blue chickens.

If you are truly serious about preparing your child for the future, don't teach him to subtract—teach him to deduct.

If you must give your child lessons, send him to driving school. He is far more likely to end up owning a Datsun than he is a Stradivarius.

Designer clothes worn by children are like snowsuits worn by adults. Few can carry it off successfully.

Never allow your child to call you by your first name. He hasn't known you long enough.

Do not elicit your child's political opinions. He doesn't know any more than you do.

Do not allow your children to mix drinks. It is unseemly and they use too much vermouth.

Don't bother discussing sex with small children. They rarely have anything to add.

Never, for effect, pull a gun on a small child. He won't get it.

Ask your child what he wants for dinner only if he's buying.

A wife invited some people to dinner. At the table, she turned to their six-year-old daughter and said, "Would you like to say the blessing?"

"I wouldn't know what to say," the girl replied.

"Just say what you hear Mommy say," the wife answered.

The daughter bowed her head and said, "Lord, why on earth did I invite all these people to dinner?"

A young boy came home from school and told his mother, "I had a big fight with Sidney. He called me a sissy."

"What did you do?" the mother asked.

"I hit him with my purse!"

"Tell me, son," the anxious mother said, "what did your father say when you told him that you'd wrecked his new Corvette?"

"Shall I leave out the swear words?" the son asked.

"Of course."

"He didn't say anything."

A three-year-old went with his dad to see a litter of kittens. On returning home, he breathlessly informed his mother there were two boy kittens and two girl kittens.

"How did you know?" his mother asked.

"Daddy picked them up and looked underneath," he replied. "I think it's printed on the bottom."

A cop got out of his car and the kid, whom he had stopped for speeding, rolled down his window. "I've been waiting for you all day," the cop said.

The kid replied, "Yeah, well I got here as fast as I could."

John invited his mother over for dinner. During the meal, his mother couldn't help noticing how beautiful John's roommate was. She had long been suspicious of a relationship between John and his roommate and this only made her more curious. Reading his mom's thoughts, John volunteered, "I know what you must be thinking, but I assure you, Julie and I are just roommates."

About a week later, Julie came to John and said, "Ever since your mother came to dinner, I've been unable to find the beautiful silver gravy ladle. You don't suppose she took it, do you?"

John said, "Well, I doubt it, but I'll write her a letter just to be sure."

So he sat down and wrote:

Dear Mother,
I'm not saying you "did" take a gravy ladle from my house, and I'm not saying you "did not" take a gravy ladle. But the fact remains that one has been missing ever since you were here for dinner.

Several days later, John received a letter from his mother which read:

Dear Son,
I'm not saying that you "do" sleep with Julie, and I'm not saying that you "do not" sleep with Julie. But the fact remains that if she was sleeping in her own bed, she would have found the gravy ladle by now.
Love, Mom

SEND IN THE HARLEQUINS
A BRIEF HISTORY OF THE CLOWN

Almost every civilization on earth has a version of the clown—a comedic character whose purpose is to entertain. There is the black-and-white-striped Hopi clown gorging on watermelon, the Aztec clowns Cortez took back to Pope Clement VII, and Viduska, the hero's servant in the Indian epic *Mahabharata*, among many others. Yet, to this day, most people think of clowns as the "whiteface" or classic clown character, such as Bozo, Ronald McDonald, or that person on the subway or bus dressed in floppy shoes toting those annoying balloons.

Although clowning goes back to ancient Egypt where a pygmy named Danga performed at the court of Pharaoh Djedkare-Isesi more than four thousand years ago, the whiteface character can be traced to sixteenth-century Italy and a popular form of theater called *commedia del'arte*. This Renaissance ancestor of comedy improv employed stock routines and characters. Among them were two "zanni" called Punchinello—who later morphed into the violent Punch (husband of the long-suffering Judy and father of the phrases "pleased as punch" and "punch line")—and Arlecchino. The roving troupes of *commedia del'arte* frequently traveled to France, where Arlecchino became Harlequin. Somewhere along the way, a white-faced character named Pierrot was added to the act.

Skipping ahead a century or so, an Englishman named Joseph Grimaldi—known as the Father of Modern Clowning—played Harlequin, but used makeup like Pierrot (to highlight his features). He incorporated sight gags and tumbling into his act, and elevated the clown's role from bit player to star. This tradition became popular in America—specifically in the American circus—through Dan Rice, a Civil War-era clown. The lanky Rice, an accomplished animal trainer, wore red, white, and blue striped tights, a top hat with stars and stripes, and a goatee. Sound familiar? Some argue that this popular circus clown (whose salary was twice that of President Lincoln) was the inspiration for Thomas Nast's Uncle Sam.

"Clowns and elephants are the pegs on which the circus is hung."
—P. T. Barnum

WE'RE HAVING MORE FUN THAN A BARREL OF MONKEYS!

1. When is a door not a door?
2. Plant the setting sun, and what will come up?
3. Why is a healthy boy like the United States?
4. What has a mouth but never eats?
5. Which is heavier: a pound of feathers or a pound of lead?
6. What is the smallest bridge in the world?
7. What can pass before the sun without making a shadow?
8. What is it that we often return and never borrow?
9. What is yours, and used by others more than yourself?
10. What is more useful when it is broken?
11. With what two animals do you always go to bed?
12. What time of day was Adam created?
13. What fur did Adam and Eve wear?
14. What is the hardest thing to deal with?

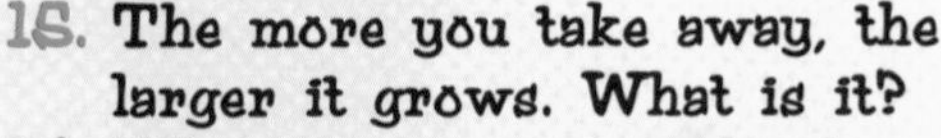

15. The more you take away, the larger it grows. What is it?
16. What increases its value by one half when turned upside down?
17. What is it that is so brittle that even to name it is to break it?

Riddles: Short & Sweet

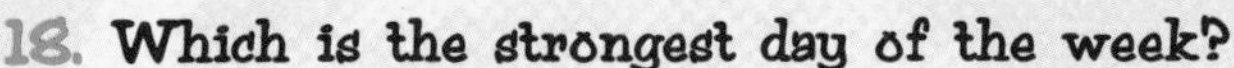
18. Which is the strongest day of the week?
19. Which travels faster—heat or cold?
20. What asks no questions but requires many answers?
21. Why is your nose not twelve inches long?
22. What is full of holes and yet holds water?
23. What do you keep even after giving it to somebody else?
24. Where did you go on your fifth birthday?
25. What falls but never breaks and breaks but never falls?
26. What is the noblest musical instrument?
27. If your uncle's sister is not your aunt, what relation is she to you?
28. What is light as a feather, nothing in it; a strong man can't hold it more than a minute?
29. What goes up and never comes down?

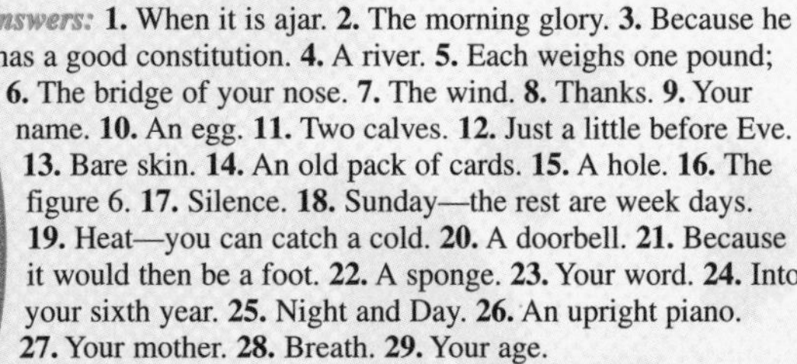
Answers: **1.** When it is ajar. **2.** The morning glory. **3.** Because he has a good constitution. **4.** A river. **5.** Each weighs one pound; **6.** The bridge of your nose. **7.** The wind. **8.** Thanks. **9.** Your name. **10.** An egg. **11.** Two calves. **12.** Just a little before Eve. **13.** Bare skin. **14.** An old pack of cards. **15.** A hole. **16.** The figure 6. **17.** Silence. **18.** Sunday—the rest are week days. **19.** Heat—you can catch a cold. **20.** A doorbell. **21.** Because it would then be a foot. **22.** A sponge. **23.** Your word. **24.** Into your sixth year. **25.** Night and Day. **26.** An upright piano. **27.** Your mother. **28.** Breath. **29.** Your age.

PNE
DUN
Nantes

Kid Friendly Jokes

Why was the tomato red?
Because it saw the salad dressing.

How do you keep a bagel from getting away?
You put lox on it.

What did one ocean say to the other ocean?
Nothing, they just waved.

What do mice do in the daytime?
Mousework.

How do you make a tissue dance?
Put a little boogie in it.

What do you get if you pour hot water down a rabbit-hole?
Hot-cross bunnies.

What did the pony say when he coughed?
"Excuse me, I'm just a little horse."

What is a raisin?
A worried grape.

Why was 6 afraid of 7?
Because 7 8 9.

What animal keeps the best time?
The watch dog.

Have you heard the joke about the watermelon?
It's pitiful.

Where would you find a prehistoric cow?
In a moo-seum.

What is black and white and red all over?
A newspaper.

Where does a general put his armies?
In his sleevies.

The Anatomy of Humor

Morris Bishop

"What is funny?" you ask, my child,
Crinkling your bright-blue eye.
"Ah, that is a curious question indeed,"
Musing, I make reply.

"Contusions are funny, not open wounds,
And automobiles that go
Crash into trees by the highwayside;
Industrial accidents, no.

"The habit of drink is a hundred per cent,
But drug addiction is nil.
A nervous breakdown will get no laughs;
Insanity surely will.

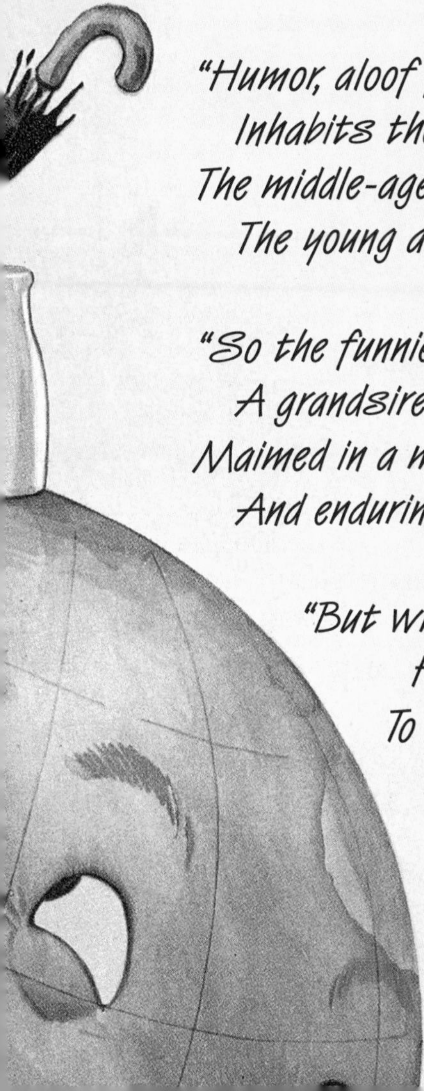

"Humor, aloof from the cigarette,
Inhabits the droll cigar;
The middle-aged are not very funny;
The young and the old, they are.

"So the funniest thing in the world should be
A grandsire, drunk, insane,
Maimed in a motor accident,
And enduring moderate pain.

"But why do you scream and yell, my child?
Here comes your mother, my honey,
To comfort you and to lecture me
For trying, she'll say, to be funny."

X-RAY GLASSES

This kooky classic has been around for decades, but the trick is still a clever one! These homemade x-ray glasses make it look like you can see a person's skeleton. Give them a try—they really work!

Materials: Ruler, 2 strips of red posterboard (2 in. by 17 in.), hole punch, black feather, white glue, 2 hardcover books, bright light

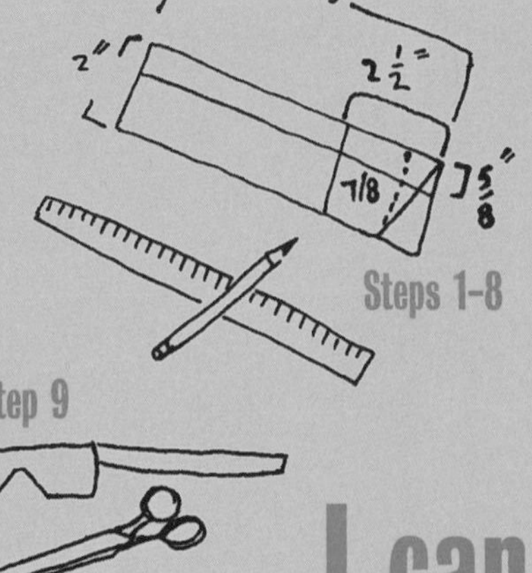

1. Fold the first strip of red posterboard in half so the 17-inch length is now 8.5 inches long.
2. Place the folded strip on a tabletop with the fold facing to your right.
3. Measure down $^5/_8$ inch from the top edge of the posterboard strip and draw a line along the length of the posterboard strip.
4. Measure $^7/_8$ inch from the right-hand fold, and draw a vertical line from top edge to bottom edge.
5. From the bottom of this line, draw a diagonal line to the top right-hand corner.
6. From the right-hand fold, measure $2^1/_2$ inches and draw a vertical line from top edge to bottom edge.

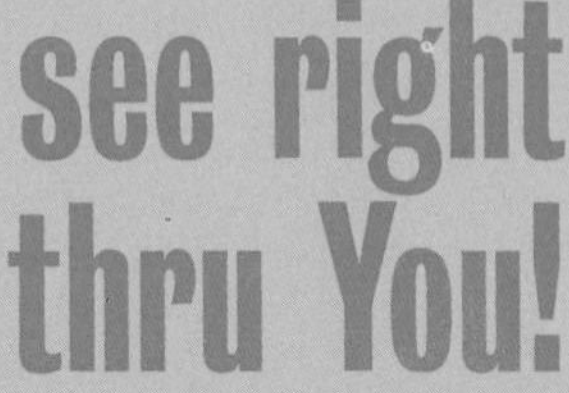

7. Cut out the large rectangle in the bottom left-hand corner, cutting through both layers of posterboard.
8. Cut out the quandrangle in the bottom right-hand corner, also cutting through both layers of posterboard.
9. Open the pair of glasses and use it to trace an identical pair of glasses on the second strip of red posterboard. Cut out the second pair of glasses.

Step 10

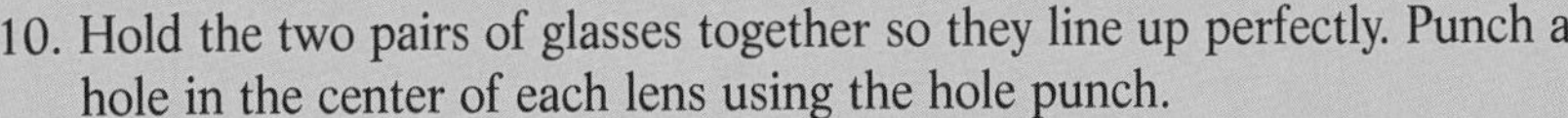

10. Hold the two pairs of glasses together so they line up perfectly. Punch a hole in the center of each lens using the hole punch.
11. Cut two pieces from the feather, each about one inch long. Glue each piece of feather to each of the red posterboard glasses so that the feathers cover the holes. Be careful not to get any glue on the part of the feather that covers each eyehole.
12. Glue the second pair of posterboard glasses to the first pair so the feathers are sandwiched between them and the holes in the lenses line up. Weigh the glasses down with hardcover books to keep them flat until the glue dries.
13. Once the glue is dry, fold back the arms of the glasses and try out the X-ray glasses. Look at your hand through the glasses under a bright light. You will see what appear to be the bones in your fingers.

Step 11

OH, LAUGHTER IS THE BEST MEDICINE!

Al Franken

As a professional comedian, I can't tell you what a relief it is to come to a chapter topic on which I have some actual expertise. Undoubtedly you have heard the expression "Laughter is the best medicine" before, and I can tell you for a fact that it isn't. Medicine is the best medicine.

Let's say you were suffering from a severe case of flesh-eating bacteria. Would you rather be treated by a doctor who would prescribe an antibiotic? Or by comedian Chris Rock, who would tell you how flesh-eating bacteria was not a problem in his neighborhood, because the bacteria were afraid of the tough motherf**kers who lived there? Funny? Indubitably. But believe me, when your lungs are turning into blood foam, the last thing you want to do is start laughing.

While clearly not the best medicine, laughter, along with chuckling, chortling, guffawing, and even the extremely mild form of amusement you are experiencing right now, has a palliative effect on your psyche. The relationship between mind and body (see Chapter 77, "Oh, Putting the Placebo Effect to Work for You!") has been firmly established in the scientific literature as the key to understanding the healing process.

In its simplest form the relationship can be illustrated this way: Good Mind = Good Body; Bad Mind = Bad Body. And what is more indicative of a good mind than a good sense of humor? A quality which, by the way, many *Playboy* Playmates claim is a turn-on, along with wearing a pukka shell necklace. If any man

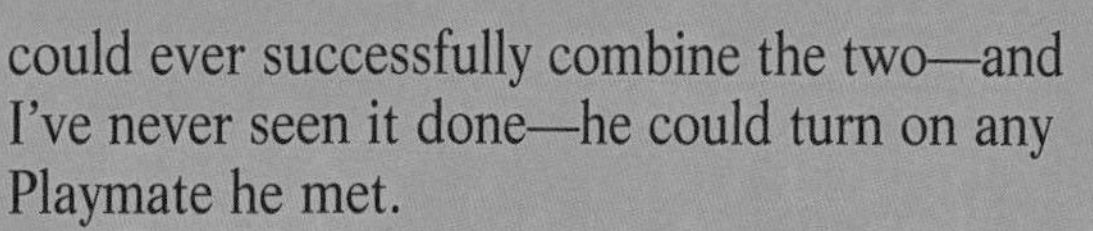

could ever successfully combine the two—and I've never seen it done—he could turn on any Playmate he met.

The effect of laughter is more than just psychological. When you laugh, your body releases endorphins, and every so often, if you laugh really hard, a small amount of diarrhea. Like a good orgasm or a good sneeze, a good laugh relieves unhealthy pent-up tensions which can cause an imbalance in the body's humors—specifically an excess of black bile—which we have known since the Middle Ages is the cause of all illness.

Beyond its clearly established physiological powers, laughing is just plain fun. Try to laugh once a day. Read this book until you laugh. Then put it down. You've laughed enough for today. Pick it up tomorrow. Continue reading, slowly and carefully to make sure you don't miss anything funny. Did you laugh? Then put the book down. For some, this book will provide a laugh a day for many years. For others, you may have to reread the book many times before you laugh even once. Don't give up. The laughs are here. You just have to find them.

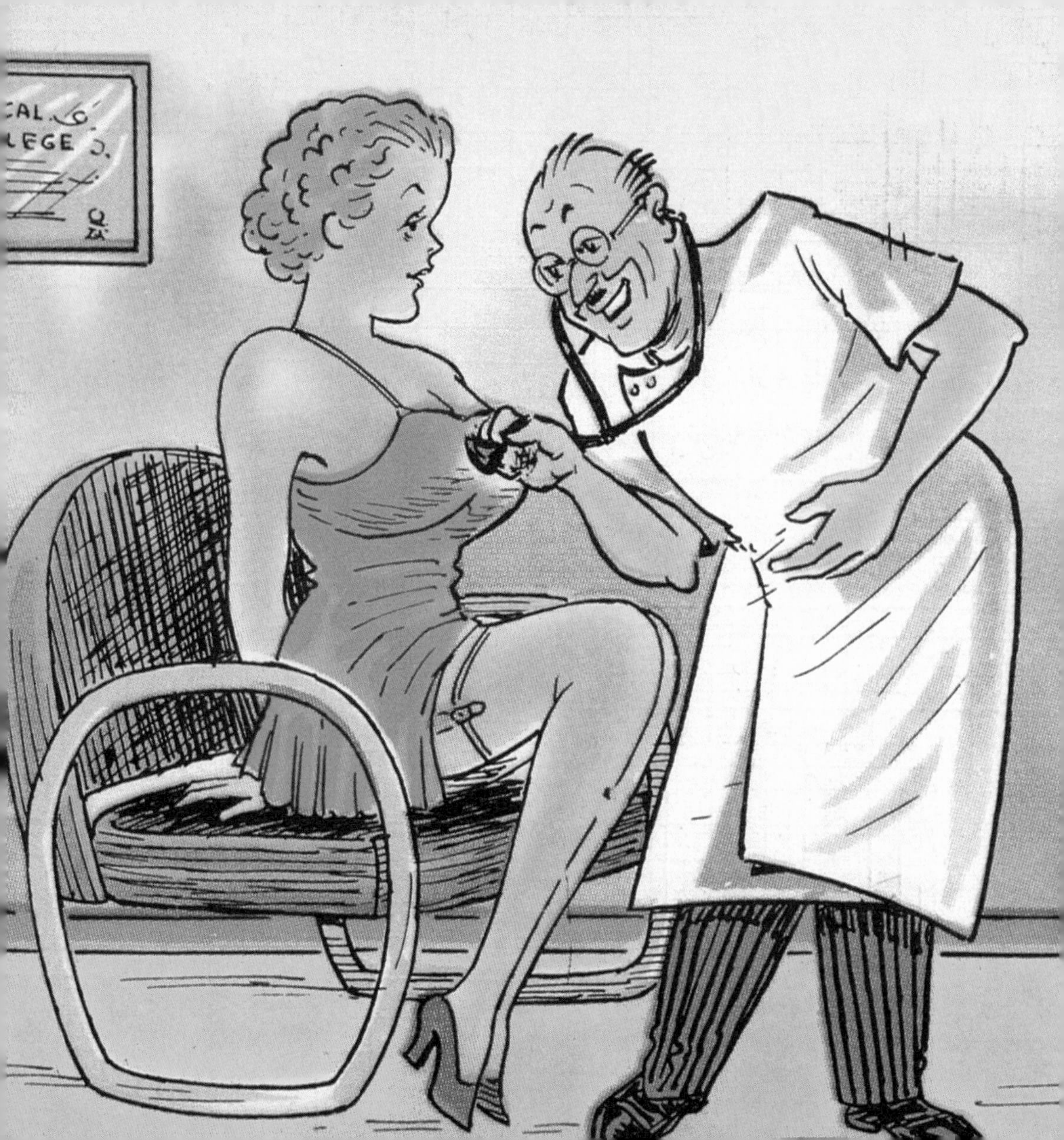

Doctor/Patient Jokes

A woman walks into the doctor's office and says, "Doctor, I hurt all over."

The doctor says, "That's impossible."

"No really!" she says, "Just look. When I touch my arm, ouch! It hurts. When I touch my leg, ouch! It hurts. When I touch my head, ouch! It hurts. When I touch my chest, ouch! It really hurts."

The doctor just shakes his head and says, "You're a natural blonde, aren't you?"

The woman smiles and says, "Why yes, I am. How did you know?"

The doctor replies, "Because your finger is broken."

A drunk goes to the doctor complaining of tiredness and headaches.

"I feel tired all the time, my head hurts, and I'm not sleeping. What is it, Doc?"

The doctor examines him thoroughly and says, "I can't find anything wrong. It must be the drinking."

"Fair enough," replies the lush. "I'll come back when you sober up."

A man walks into a dentist's office and says, "Excuse me, can you help me. I think I'm a moth."

Dentist: "You don't need a dentist. You need a psychiatrist."

Man: "Yes, I know."

Dentist: "So why did you come in here?"

Man: "The light was on … "

A middle-aged woman has a heart attack and is taken to the hospital. While on the operating table she has a near death experience.

Seeing God, she asks, "Is my time up?"

God answers, "No, you have

Doctor: "I've got very bad news – you've got cancer and Alzheimer's."
Patient: "Well, at least I don't have cancer."

another 40 years, 2 months and 8 days to live."

Upon recovery, the woman decides to stay in the hospital and have a face-lift, liposuction, and a tummy tuck. She even has someone come in and change her hair color. Since she has so much more time to live, she figures, she might as well make the most of it.

After her last operation, she is released from the hospital. While crossing the street on her way home, she is hit by a car and dies immediately.

Arriving in front of God, she demands, "I thought you said I had another 40 years, why didn't you pull me from out of the path of the car?"

God replies, "I didn't recognize you."

A psychiatrist is conducting a group therapy session with three young mothers and their small children. "You all have obsessions," he observes.

To the first mother, he says, "You are obsessed with eating. You've even named your daughter Candy."

He turns to the second mom. "Your obsession is money. Again, it manifests itself in your child's name, Penny."

At this point, the third mother gets up, takes her little boy by the hand and whispers, "Come on, Dick, let's go."

A couple who is having trouble getting pregnant goes to see a doctor. The doctor gives the man a revolutionary new injection made from monkey glands, which works perfectly. Nine months and two weeks later, his wife has a baby. When the nurse comes out of the delivery room with the news, the man asks, "Is it a boy or a girl?" And the nurse replies, "We won't know until it comes down off the light fixtures."

Three doctors die and go to heaven where they are met by St. Peter at the pearly gates.

Peter asks the first one what he did on earth, and he says he was an obstetrician who had brought hundreds of babies into the world. So St. Peter says, "Excellent, you can go in to heaven."

The second doctor says he was a pediatrician and explains that he cared for and healed thousands of sick children. St. Peter says, "Sounds very useful, very good. You can go in, too."

The third doctor says he was president of a HMO conglomerate. Peter asks what that means, and the man explains his job.

"All right," says Peter, "You can go in, too, but you can only stay three days."

A man hasn't been feeling well, so he goes to his doctor for a complete check-up. Later, the doctor comes out with the results.

"I'm afraid I have some very bad news," the doctor says. "You're dying, and you don't have much time left."

"Oh, that's terrible!" says the man. "How long have I got?"

"Ten," the doctor says sadly.

"Ten?" the man asks. "Ten what? Months? Weeks? Days?"

The doctor interrupts, "Nine . . ."

YOU'D BETTER LEAVE NO
HIS TEMPERATURE KEEPS GOI

– UP!

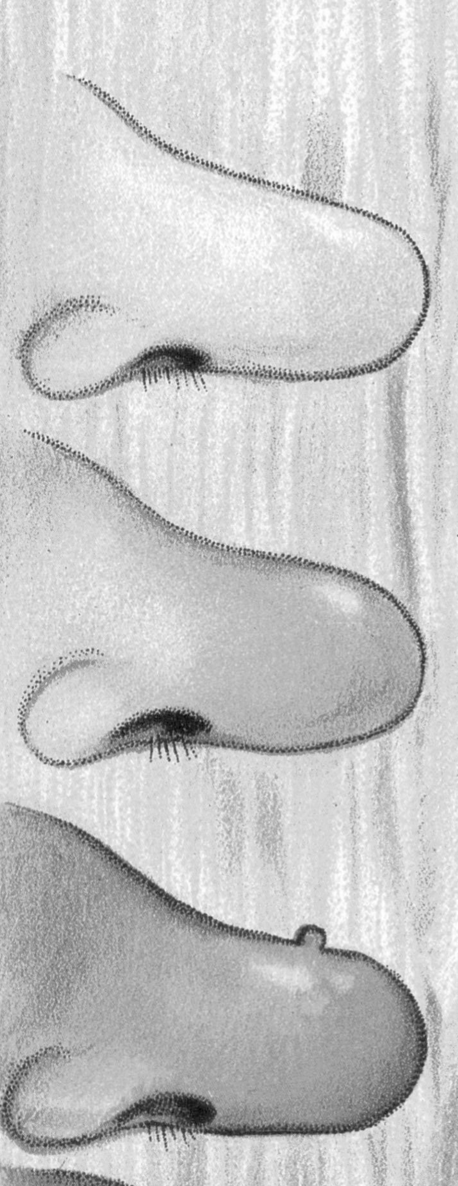

The Common Cold

Ogden Nash

Go hang yourself, you old M.D.!
You shall no longer sneer at me.
Pick up your hat and stethoscope,
Go wash your mouth with laundry soap;
I contemplate a joy exquisite
In never paying you for your visit.
I did not call you to be told
My malady is a common cold.

By pounding brow and swollen lip;
By fever's hot and scaly grip;
By these two red redundant eyes
That weep like woeful April skies;
By racking snuffle, snort, and sniff;
By handkerchief after handkerchief;
This cold you wave away as naught
Is the damnedest cold man ever caught.

Give ear, you scientific fossil!
Here is the genuine Cold Colossal;
The Cold of which researchers dream,

The Perfect Cold, the Cold Supreme.
This honored system humbly holds
The Super-cold to end all colds;
The Cold Crusading for Democracy;
The Führer of the Streptococcracy.

Bacilli swarm within my portals
Such as were ne'er conceived by mortals,
But bred by scientists wise and hoary
In some Olympian laboratory;
Bacteria as large as mice,
With feet of fire and heads of ice
Who never interrupt for slumber
Their stamping elephantine rumba.

A common cold, forsooth, gadzooks!
Then Venus showed promise of good looks;
Don Juan was a budding gallant,
And Shakespeare's plays show signs of talent;
The Arctic winter is rather coolish,
And your diagnosis is fairly foolish.
Oh what derision history holds
For the man who belittled the Cold of Colds!

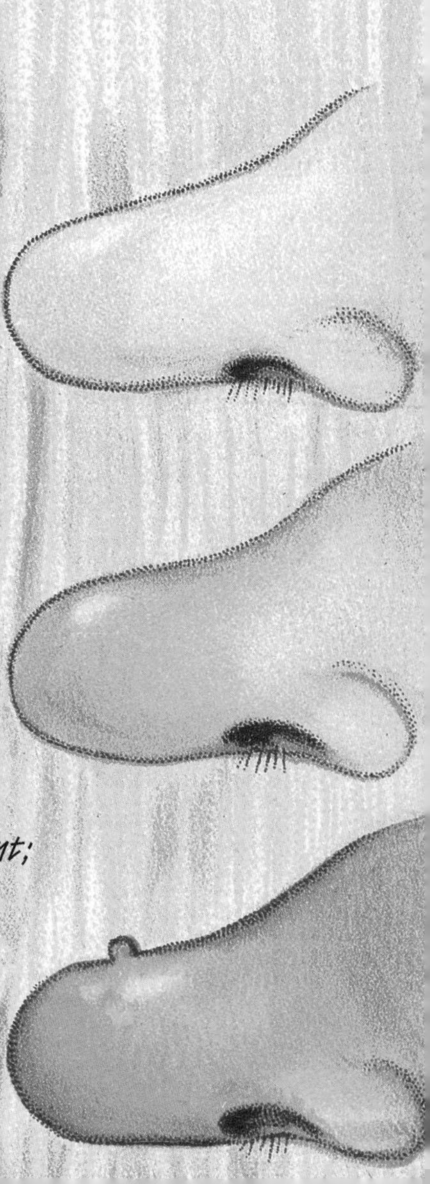

WAITING ROOMS

Jerry Seinfeld

I hate the waiting room because it's called the waiting room so there's no chance of not waiting. It's built, designed, and intended for waiting. Why would they take you right away when they've got this room all set up? And you sit there with your little magazine. You pretend you're reading it but you're really looking at the other people. "I wonder what he's got." Then they finally call you, and you think you're going to see the doctor, but you're not. You're going into the next smaller waiting room. Now you don't even have your magazine. You've got no pants on. You're looking at colon cancer brochures, peeking out the blinds.

But medically speaking, it's always good to be in a small room. You don't want to be in a large room. Have you ever seen these operating theaters that they have with stadium seating? You don't want them doing anything to you that makes other doctors go, "Well, I have to see this. Are you kidding? Are they really going to do that? Are there seats? Can we get in?"

I wonder if they ever scalp tickets to an operation? "I got two for the Winslow tumor, who needs two?"

(By the way, don't think I didn't see the scalp tickets-scalpel joke opportunity. I just passed. If you'd like to make one, be my guest.)

Classic Comics
Baseball is 90% mental,
the other half is physical.

Classic Comics

This is like déjà vu all over again. Slump? I ain't in no slump. I just ain't hittin'. You can observe a lot just by watching. You better cut the pizza in four pieces because I'm not hungry enough to eat six. If you come to a fork in the road, take it. I always thought that record would stand until it was broken. You should always go to other people's funerals; otherwise, they won't come to yours. I'm not going to buy my kids an encyclopedia. Let them walk to school like I did. Half the lies they tell about me aren't true. It gets late early out here. The other teams could make trouble for us if they win. You wouldn't have won if we'd beaten you. It's tough to make predictions, especially about the future. A nickel isn't worth a dime today. I didn't really say everything I said.

Yogi Berra

A Hall of Fame baseball player and former coach, Yogi Berra is known as much for his amazing stats as he is for his ditzy and unintentionally funny comments. Berra's career as a player and coach in baseball spanned some fifty years, during which he was a fifteen-time All Star, three-time MVP, and holder of the record for the most times on a winning World Series team. As a catcher, Yogi was always known as a big talker, chatting it up with batters at the plate in an effort to distract them. With sayings like these, you can imagine why he was so successful!

REAL Funny

EATING CROW: SPORTS & ENTERTAINMENT

Actual statements and comments made by various people throughout history

"Walt Whitman is as unacquainted with art as a hog is with mathematics."
— *The London Critic*, 1855

"I'm sorry Mr. Kipling, but you just don't know how to use the English language."
— Editor of the *San Francisco Examiner*, responding to a submission by Rudyard Kipling, 1889

"Who would want to see a play about an unhappy traveling salesman? Too depressing."
— Broadway producer, Cheryl Crawford, rejecting an offer to stage Arthur Miller's *Death of a Salesman*, 1948

"Who the hell wants to hear actors talk?"
— H. M. Warner of Warner Brothers, about the advent of the "talkies," 1927

"[I]t will be gone by June."
— comment on the staying power of rock 'n roll, *Variety*, 1955

"Can't act. Can't sing. Balding. Can dance a little."
— MGM executive, evaluating Fred Astaire's screen test, 1928

"Reagan doesn't have the presidential look."
— United Artists executive, rejecting Ronald Reagan for the starring role in the movie *The Best Man*, 1964

"Displays no trace of imagination, good taste or ingenuity. I say it's a stinkeroo."
— *New Yorker* critic Russell Maloney, reviewing *The Wizard of Oz*, August 19, 1939

"[J]ust so-so in center field."
— *New York Daily News*, assessing the talents of New York Giants' Willie Mays after his major-league debut, May 26, 1951

"Kid, you're too small. You ought to go out and shine shoes."
— Casey Stengel, manager of the Brooklyn Dodgers, turning down Phil Rizzuto after a Dodger tryout, 1936

"We don't like their sound, and guitar music is on the way out."
— Decca Recording Co., rejecting the Beatles, 1962

"Far too noisy, my dear Mozart. Far too many notes."

— Emperor Ferdinand of Austria, after the first performance of *The Marriage of Figaro*, May 1, 1786

A flatulent soprano
named Dotty

Had a luncheon of
beans and biscotti

Then, I'm sad
to impart,

Her intestines
took part

In her duet
with poor
Pavarotti

Laughable Limericks

I sat next to the Duchess at tea,
Distressed as a person could be.
Her rumblings abdominal
Were simply phenomenal—
And everyone thought it was me!

A collegiate damsel named Breeze,
Weighed down by B.A.'s and Litt. D.'s
Collapsed from the strain.
Alas, it was plain
She was killing herself by degrees.

A sensitive girl named O'Neill
Once went up in the big Ferris Wheel;
But when halfway around
She looked down at the ground,
And it cost her a two-dollar meal.

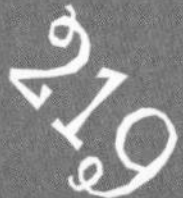

PASSING GAS

Whoopi Goldberg

We all fart, right? We all get that cramp that tells us there's an air bubble percolating in our butt and it needs to escape. But we don't like to talk about it. Everybody does it, and no one talks about it. Why is that?

...For the most part, a fart is a fart. We feel it coming. We know what it is. And we usually have enough butt control to drop 'em at will, or hold 'em back for a more appropriate time, or ease 'em out slow and silent. The game is in figuring out which approach to take, and then what to do with yourself after you've made your deposit.

I'm a great believer in claiming farts. Always have, always will. I don't want to be blamed for one of yours.

...I think there should be some sort of code word, some way to politely signal that you're got some business going on. It's common courtesy. I always call my farts tree monkeys, 'cause tree monkeys make the same farty sound as I do. It's a funny little sound. It would almost be cute, if it wasn't followed by the smell. It's like lightning and thunder. You get that funny little sound, and then the smell hits you. Sometimes it takes a few beats; sometimes it hits you right away. I just say, "Tree monkey," then I get up and walk away. I don't wait for it to hit. I go to the other end of the room and let people figure it out for themselves.

TAOISM
Shit happens.

CONFUCIANISM
Confucious say,
"Shit happens."

BUDDHISM
If shit happens, it
isn't really shit.

MYSTICISM
This is some really weird shit.

HINDUISM
This shit has happened before.

CATHOLICISM
If shit happens,
you deserve it.

ATHEISM
What shit?

PROTESTANTISM
Let shit happen
to someone else.

Shit Happens in Various Religions

ISLAM
If shit happens, it is the will of Allah.

ZEN
What is the sound of shit happening?

JUDAISM
Why does shit always happen to US?

LUTHERANISM
If shit happens, just don't talk about it.

HEDONISM
There's nothing like a good shit happening.

RASTAFARIANISM
Let's roll up that shit and smoke it.

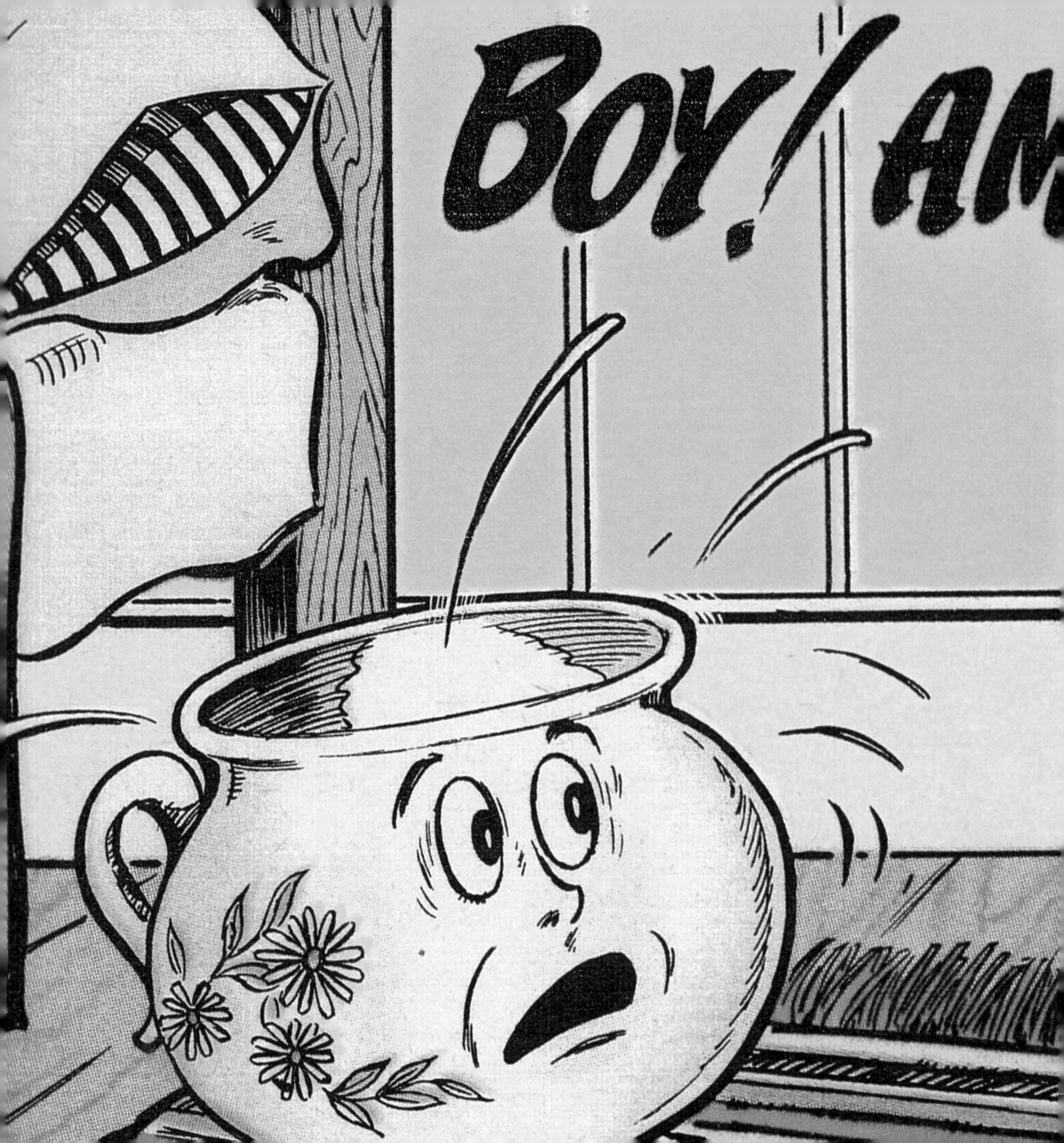
BOY! AM

I POOPED!

WHY MAN INVENTED THE VIDEO CAMERA

Ray Romano

As your child gets older, the diaper stage takes on a whole different dynamic.

If you've ever seen a kid poop in his diaper *standing up*, you know what I'm talking about. If you ask me, it's why man invented the video camera.

It's quite a funny sight. And you can always tell when it's happening.

When everything's normal, they're running around the room at a hundred miles an hour. It's when you catch that sudden slowdown in the action that you know it's time to plug in the Handycam.

Suddenly, instead of running, they're walking. Then they're pacing, and finally they come to a complete stop. Just standing in one spot. Although in some instances you might be able to detect a slight rocking.

Then they get an odd look on their face. It's sort of a slight grimace with a "why me" in their eyes. The back arches a little. And then the dead giveaway, the shuffle behind the furniture.

If you see your diaper-clad child with that face on, wedged into a little nook and cranny somewhere behind the couch, it's *go time*.

In some cases you might witness what I call "the Leaner." It's everything mentioned above, with a little extra strain in his face as he bends over slightly at the waist, putting one hand on the couch arm for support.

Never make eye contact with "the Leaner." He's like a pit bull, and if he sees you looking at him, you're going to get a face full of growl.

"ARRRRRRRRRRGH! ARRRRRR-RRRRRRRRRRRRRRRRRRRRRRR!"

Oddly enough, as an adult, things really don't change that much. Sure, you probably don't have people watching you, but there's always some idiot knocking on the bathroom door. You still growl, only now it's:

"I'M IN HERE!"

Did you hear about the Buddhist who refused his dentist's Novocain during root canal work?
—He wanted to transcend dental medication.

Did you hear about the Old Testament hooker who was arrested for trying to make a Prophet?

A mushroom walked into a bar and announced:
"The drinks are on me."
The bartender said: "Why are you buying everybody drinks?"
"Because I'm a fungi."

What do you have if you have 20 rabbits all in a row and they all back up one step?
— A receding hare-line.

Two atoms ran into each other. One atom said:
"I think I've lost an electron."
The second atom said: "Are you sure?"
The first atom said: "I'm positive."

Did you hear about the man who fell into an upholstery machine?
— He's fully recovered.

If you are American when you go into a toilet and you are American when you come out of the toilet, what are you while you are in the toilet?

— *European, of course.*

There was a young
lady named Harris

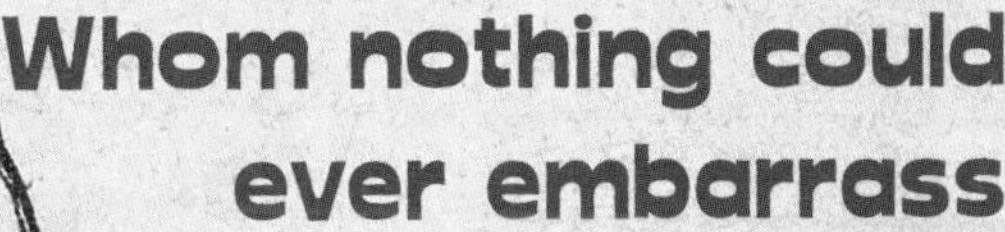

Whom nothing could
ever embarrass

'Til the salts
that she shook

In the bath
that she took

Turned out to be
Plaster of Paris.

REAL Funny

SOAP SAGA

The following is an actual correspondence between a London hotel's staff and one of its guests. The London hotel involved submitted this to The Sunday Times.

Dear Maid,
Please do not leave any more of those little bars of soap in my bathroom since I have brought my own bath-sized Dial. Please remove the six unopened little bars from the shelf under the medicine chest and another three in the shower soap dish. They are in my way. Thank you,

S. Berman

Dear Room 635,
I am not your regular maid. She will be back tomorrow, Thursday, from her day off. I took the 3 hotel soaps out of the shower soap dish as you requested. The 6 bars on your shelf I took out of your way and put on top of your Kleenex dispenser in case you should change your mind. This leaves only the 3 bars I left today which my instructions from the management is to leave 3 soaps daily.

I hope this is satisfactory.

Kathy, Relief Maid

Dear Maid,
I hope you are my regular maid,

Apparently Kathy did not tell you about my note to her concerning the little bars of soap. When I got back to my room this evening I found you had added 3 little Camays to the shelf under my medicine cabinet.

I am going to be here in the hotel for two weeks and have brought my own bath-size Dial so I won't need those 6 little Camays which are on the shelf. They are in my way when shaving, brushing teeth, etc.

Please remove them.

S. Berman

Dear Mr. Berman,
The assistant manager, Mr. Kensedder, informed me this A.M. that you called him last evening and said you were unhappy with your maid service. I have assigned a new girl to your room. I

MINER
SOAP

hope you will accept my apologies for any past inconvenience. If you have any future complaints please contact me so I can give it my personal attention. Call extension 11:08 between 8 A.M. and 5 P.M. Thank you.

Elaine Carmen, Housekeeper

Dear Miss Carmen,
It is impossible to contact you by phone since I leave the hotel for business at 7:45 A.M. and don't get back before 5:30 or 6 P.M. That's the reason I called Mr. Kensedder last night. You were already off duty.

I only asked Mr. Kensedder if he could do anything about those little bars of soap. The new maid you assigned me must have thought I was a new check-in today, since she left another 3 bars of hotel soap in my medicine cabinet along with her regular delivery of 3 bars on the bathroom shelf. In just 5 days here I have accumulated 24 little bars of soap. Why are you doing this to me?

S. Berman

Dear Mr. Berman,
Your maid, Kathy, has been instructed to stop delivering soap to your room and remove the extra soaps.

Thank you,
Elaine Carmen, Housekeeper

Dear Mr. Kensedder,
My bath-size Dial is missing. Every bar of soap was taken from my room including my own bath-size Dial. I came in late last night and had to call the bellhop to bring me 4 little Cashmere Bouquets.

S. Berman

Dear Mr. Berman,
I have informed our housekeeper, Elaine Carmen, of your soap problem.

I cannot understand why there was no soap in your room since our maids are instructed to leave 3 bars of soap each time they service a room. The situation will be rectified immediately. Please accept my apologies for the inconvenience.

Martin L. Kensedder
Assistant Manager

Dear Mrs. Carmen,
Who the hell left 54 little bars of Camay in my room? I came in last night and found 54 little bars of soap. I don't want 54 little bars of Camay. All I want is my bath-size Dial.

Please give me back my bath-size Dial.

S. Berman

Dear Mr. Berman,
You complained of too much soap in your room so I had them removed.

Then you complained to Mr. Kensedder that all your soap was missing so I personally returned them. Obviously your maid, Kathy, did not know I had returned your soaps so she also brought 24 Camays plus the 3 daily Camays. I don't know where you got the idea this hotel issues bath-size Dial. I was able to locate some bath-size Ivory which I left in your room.

Elaine Carmen, Housekeeper

Dear Mrs. Carmen,
Just a short note to bring you up-to-date on my latest soap inventory.

As of today I possess:

- On shelf under medicine cabinet—18 Camay in 4 stacks of 4 and 1 stack of 2.
- On Kleenex dispenser—11 Camay in 2 stacks of 4 and 1 stack of 3.
- On bedroom dresser—1 stack of 3 Cashmere Bouquet, 1 stack of 4 hotel-size Ivory, and 8 Camay in 2 stacks of 4.
- Inside medicine cabinet—14 Camay in 3 stacks of 4 and 1 stack of 2.
- In shower soap dish — 6 Camay, very moist.
- On northeast corner of tub—1 Cashmere Bouquet, slightly used.
- On northwest corner of tub—6 Camays in 2 stacks of 3.

Please ask Kathy when she services my room to make sure the stacks are neatly piled and dusted. Also, please advise her that stacks of more than 4 have a tendency to tip. May I suggest that my bedroom windowsill is not in use and will make an excellent spot for future soap deliveries. One more item, I have purchased another bar of bath-sized Dial which I am keeping in the hotel vault in order to avoid further misunderstandings.

S. Berman

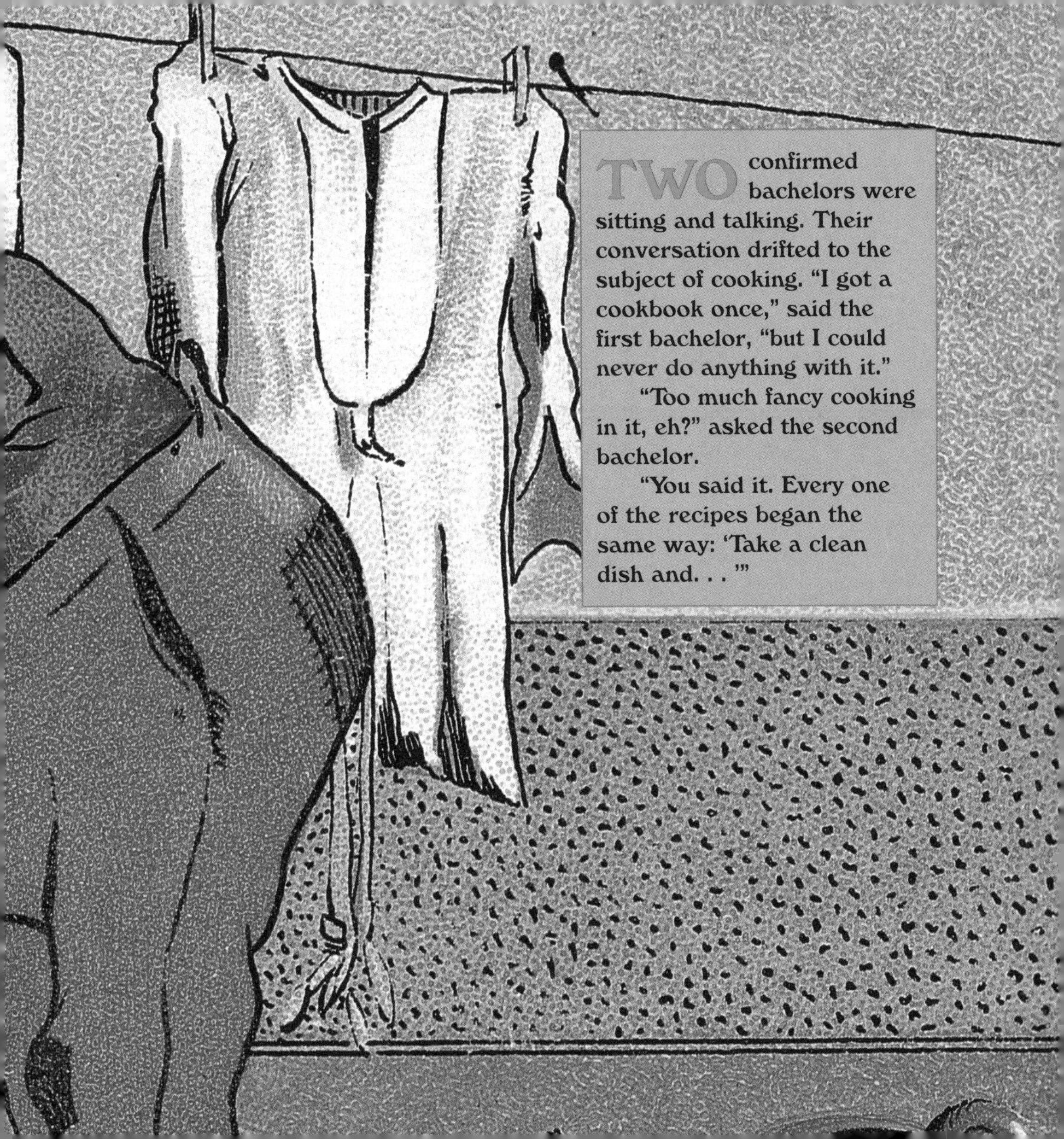
TWO confirmed bachelors were sitting and talking. Their conversation drifted to the subject of cooking. "I got a cookbook once," said the first bachelor, "but I could never do anything with it."
"Too much fancy cooking in it, eh?" asked the second bachelor.
"You said it. Every one of the recipes began the same way: 'Take a clean dish and. . . '"

How to Shower Like a Woman

1. Take off clothing and place it in sectioned laundry hamper according to lights and darks.
2. Walk to bathroom wearing long robe. If you see husband along the way, modestly cover up exposed areas.
3. Look at your womanly physique in the mirror—make mental note to do more sit-ups.
4. Get in the shower. Use face cloth, arm cloth, leg cloth, loofah, and pumice stone.
5. Wash your hair once with vitamin enriched cucumber and sage shampoo.
6. Condition your hair with grapefruit mint conditioner enhanced with natural avocado oil. Leave on hair for 5 minutes before rinsing.
7. Wash your face with crushed apricot facial scrub.
8. Wash rest of body with ginger nut and jaffa cake body wash.
9. Shave armpits and legs.
10. Turn off shower.
11. Squeegee off all wet surfaces in shower.
12. Get out of shower. Dry with towel the size of a small country. Wrap hair in super absorbent towel.
13. Check entire body for zits. Tweeze all unwanted hairs.
14. Mosturize entire face and body with vanilla-scented lotion.
15. Return to bedroom wearing long robe and towel on head. If you see husband along the way, cover up any exposed areas.

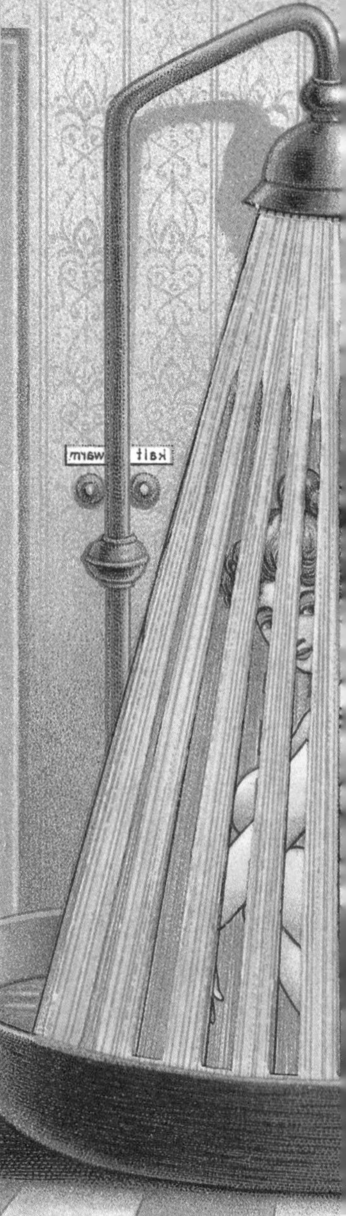

Jokes

How to Shower Like a Man

1. Take off clothes and leave them in a pile on the floor.
2. Walk naked to the bathroom. If you see wife along the way, shake wiener at her, making the "woo-woo" sound.
3. Look at your manly physique in the mirror. Admire the size of your wiener and scratch your butt.
4. Get in the shower.
5. Wash your face.
6. Wash your armpits.
7. Blow your nose in your hands and let the water rinse them off.
8. Make fart noises (real or artificial) and laugh at how loud they sound in the shower.
9. Spend majority of time washing privates and surrounding area.
10. Wash your butt.
11. Shampoo your hair. Make a shampoo mohawk.
12. Pee.
13. Rinse off and get out of shower.
14. Partially dry off. Fail to notice water on floor due to curtain hanging out of tub the whole time.
15. Admire wiener size in mirror again.
16. Return to bedroom with towel around your waist. If you pass wife, pull off towel, shake wiener at her and make the "woo-woo" sound again.
17. Throw wet towel on bed.

TIM AL-LAND

Tim Allen

Conventional wisdom says that if you want something done well you should do it yourself. So I've decided to design my own amusement park. It will be the ultimate men's zone.

I'll call it Tim Al-Land.

Men are fascinated by, preoccupied with, and genetically predisposed toward two things: Construction and Destruction. Think of the stuff that boys do. Build and destroy. Nothing's changed.

Women are invited to Tim Al-Land, but as with most men's zones, women just don't want to go there. It smells like feet and body odor. It's not real comfortable. It's comfortable *enough*, if you're the kind of guy who likes spending all day on a park bench. It's also chilly all the time, and loud.

Throughout the park there are signs posting rules, which, when broken, earn you a free food ticket. The food pavilions serve the basic men's food groups: meat, carbohydrates, salt, and fat. The hot dogs are rubbery and the potato chips stale. Everything's cooked on a fire and shoved into a casing. All beverages are ice cold. All the tables are tailgates. In the bathrooms there are no toilet seats. But there is a recorded voice that cycles through, "Can't you remember to put the seat down when you're through? How hard can it be? I don't find it funny. I almost fell in…" It always gets a big laugh from the married guys. There aren't even any women's bathrooms.

You gotta walk through a big drill to get into Tim Al-Land.

"There's your armature right there. Your pinion's there, son. Stand by the trigger and I'll take your picture."

Inside, you have to wear a vest with lots of pockets. If you forget yours we provide them, just like fancy restaurants when they require coats and ties and you come dressed like a bozo.

As the creator of Tim Al-Land, I suggest the ladies just leave their men at the gate and take advantage of the complete beauty makeover offered at the Tim Al-Land Ladies Annex across the street. Our motto: "We'll make sure it takes hours. And all your girlfriends will be there."

Tim Al-Land: Maybe I can get Disney to do this.

The park reflects the best and worst in man, and is divided into zones. The first is Constructionland.

In Constructionland, you can frame a house. Hell, you can put up a barn. You can lay brick. You can build a bridge. I don't know any guy in the world who wouldn't spend twenty-two bucks for a ticket to run a backhoe all day long. Learn how a front-end loader works. Drive a bulldozer, a grader. You get training in a big gravel pit. Seven bucketloads and you're outta there, so the next guy can get a turn.

Next to the gravel pit is a special place where you can use big metal jaws hanging from a crane to try to pick up a car and put it down a little chute. Get it down the chute, it's yours. Damage it and it's yours, too. Of course you damage it!

Even though blowing up things requires the same energy and creativity as building things, Destructionland is clearly the dark side of man.

In Destructionland, a.k.a. Militaryland, men get to use all that Army stuff:

machine guns, howitzers, tanks. Only this time they're real. Remember that bridge you built? Blow it up!

In Militaryland you can also sit on the deck of the USS *Missouri*—now decommissioned—and shoot a sixty-inch gun. The shells go twenty miles and, if aimed properly, will obliterate your neighbor's house and leave yours standing.

There would have to be some sort of beer pavilion for refreshments. Something with a Bavarian theme, like the Obermeyer Tent. Waitresses in halter tops and lederhosen. Beer steins with relief maps of Italy on them. We could sit around and try to figure out why the Bavarians made cups with metal caps that serve no useful purpose.

After you quench your thirst, it's into the men's room. It's all trough. Forty feet long. The trough of hell. Solid aluminum. Water sloshing through. Eighty guys lined up like horses. And the stalls: no doors, just holes in the floor, like in Italy. No woman would understand it.

Finally, it's off to Fishingland. Full of fish things. You can see fish, touch fish, kiss fish. Even feel what it's like to be hooked.

"Hold still, kid."

"Oh, god that hurts!" Oh, sonofabitch that hurts!"

"Try *that!*"

"Oh, jeez, you're right, that hook really hurts. Isn't that great!"

After all the fun at Tim Al-Land, it's finally time to go.

There's a bar next door to the Ladies' Annex where you can grab a beer just in case your wife's hair still isn't done.

But please, no firing the sixty-millimeter guns at the Annex.

comics

You might be a redneck if...

...you've been on television more than 5 times describing what a tornado sounded like.

...you've ever cut your grass and found a car.

...you've ever had to haul a can of paint to the top of a water tower to defend your sister's honor.

...every day somebody comes to your door mistakenly thinking you're having a yard sale.

...you've ever made change in the offering plate.

...you see a sign that says "Say no to crack" and it reminds you to pull your jeans up.

...going to the bathroom in the middle of the night involves shoes and a flashlight.

...your two-year-old has more teeth than you do.

...you've ever spray painted your girlfriend's name on an overpass.

...you consider a six-pack of beer and a bug zapper quality entertainment.

...your junior-senior prom had a day-care center.

...your pocketknife often doubles as a toothpick.

...your dog and your wallet are both on a chain.

...your family tree does not fork.

...you have a Hefty Bag for a passenger-side window.

...you view duct tape as a long-term investment.

...you've ever worn a tube top to a wedding.

...you go to the family reunion to meet women.

Jeff Foxworthy

Known for his Southern brand of humor, Jeff Foxworthy made it chic to be "hick"! Inspired by the irony of a bowling alley with valet parking, Foxworthy dreamed up his uproarious "You might be a redneck if…" routine, lampooning the stereotypes of the South. Counting himself among the "rednecks" he made fun of, he parlayed his stage success into starring in his own sitcom, The Jeff Foxworthy Show, *authoring numerous best-selling books, and producing Grammy-winning CDs that have sold more than any other recording comic artist in history.*

What do you call a guy who has no arms and no legs but is a great swimmer?
—Bob

Jokes

What do you call a guy...

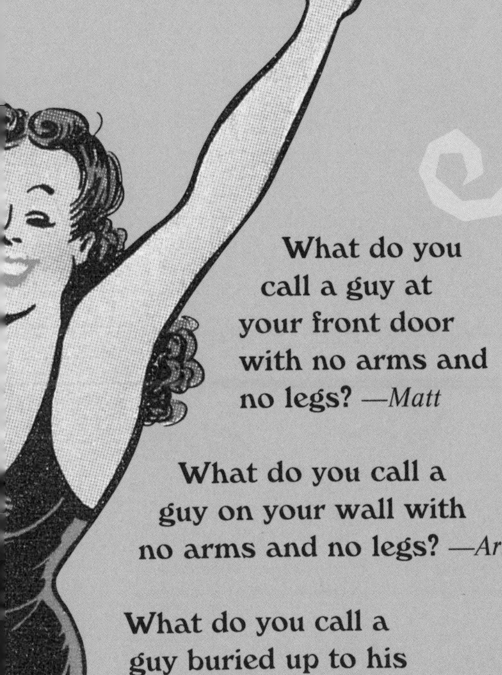

What do you call a guy at your front door with no arms and no legs? *—Matt*

What do you call a guy on your wall with no arms and no legs? *—Art*

What do you call a guy buried up to his neck with no arms and no legs? *—Spike*

What do you call a guy water skiing with no arms and no legs? *—Skip*

What do you call a guy in a pile of leaves with no arms and no legs? *—Russell*

What do you call a guy in a meat grinder with no arms and no legs? *—Chuck*

What do you call a guy stuffed in a mailbox with no arms and no legs? *—Bill*

What do you call a guy in a flower pot with no arms and no legs? *—Pete*

What do you call a guy in a pot of boiling water with no arms and no legs?*—Stu*

What do you call two guys on your wall with no arms and no legs?*—Kurt and Rod*

Simple GAGS

SUGAR SWAP Replace the contents of the sugar bowl with antacid. When someone puts sugar in their coffee it will start to foam and overflow.

SINK SPRAY Slip a rubber band around the sink sprayer handle so that it is fully depressed. Place it back in the cradle with the nozzle facing out. When your victim turns on the sink faucet, they will get a very wet surprise!

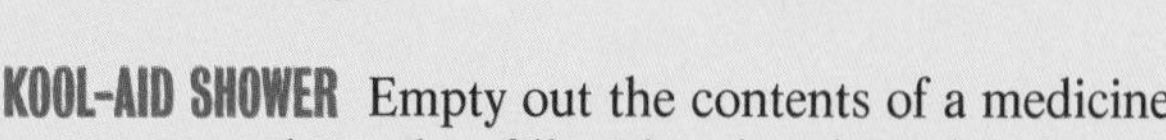

KOOL-AID SHOWER Empty out the contents of a medicine capsule, and re-fill with colored Kool-Aid powder. Unscrew the showerhead, place the capsule inside and screw back on. When the shower is turned on, the water will dissolve the gel cap and voila! — it's a colorful Kool-Aid shower!

CONFETTI FOG Climb a ladder and dump a bunch of confetti on top of the blades of your victim's ceiling fan. When they turn on the fan, a cloud of confetti will descend.

CONFETTI RAIN Turn your victim's umbrella upside down, fill it with confetti, close it up, and snap or Velcro it tightly shut. Wait until a rainy day and enjoy.

SUD-LESS SOAP Paint all the bars of soap in your house with transparent nail polish and replace them in the soap dishes. This keeps the soap from lathering, no matter how hard you rub it.

THE UNDERWEAR SCARE Sew all your victim's underwear together! Just use one or two stitches at each the seam and replace them in the drawer. When they pull out a pair of underwear, they will keep coming out in an endless line.

THE IMMOVABLE COIN Superglue several quarters to a flat surface such as a bench or floor and watch people try unsuccessfully to pick them up.

TOOTHPASTE TOMFOOLERY Squirt a little toothpaste on the underside of light switches and doorknobs.

RISE AND SHINE! Wait until your family has gone to bed and are all sleeping soundly. Pull all the shades down and close all the curtains in the house. Reset all the clocks, including the alarm clocks for four hours earlier. When the alarm(s) go off at 3 A.M. instead of 7 A.M., just get up and ready, as usual. Wait until the whole family is seated at the breakfast table groggily eating and ask one of them to look out the nearest window. When they pull back the curtain, they will find a night sky and a sign posted to the window that says "Gotcha! It's only 3 A.M.! Go back to sleep!"

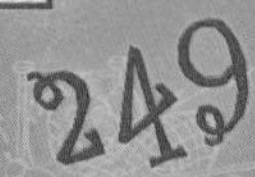

Anagram	Answer
HAS TO PILFER	SHOPLIFTER
MOON STARER	ASTRONOMER
EVIL'S AGENT	EVANGELIST
A ROPE ENDS IT	DESPERATION
HERE COME DOTS	THE MORSE CODE
CASH LOST IN 'EM	SLOT MACHINES
WOMAN HITLER	MOTHER-IN-LAW
I'M A DOT IN PLACE	A DECIMAL POINT
THAT QUEER SHAKE	THE EARTHQUAKES
ACCORD NOT IN IT	CONTRADICTION
NINE THUMPS	PUNISHMENT
VOICES RANT ON	CONVERSATION
HEY, DOG, RUN!	GREYHOUND
NO CITY DUST HERE	THE COUNTRYSIDE
BOTTOMS UP!	PUBS' MOTTO
MAD POLICY	DIPLOMACY
SIGNS: POOR	PROGNOSIS
IS NO MEAL	SEMOLINA
A CENT TIP	PITTANCE
SOW IT, LAD	WILD OATS
IS NO AMITY	ANIMOSITY
DIRTY ROOM	DORMITORY

ALAS! NO MORE Z'S

Answer: Snooze alarms

Celebrity Anagrams...

SO I'M CUTER .... TOM CRUISE
MERRY WARDROBE .... DREW BARRYMORE
OLD WEST ACTION .... CLINT EASTWOOD
BOGART GEAR .... GRETA GARBO
A PAL ICON .... AL PACINO
UTTER NERD .... TED TURNER
BIG RALLY HAM .... BILLY GRAHAM
HE DROWNS ART .... HOWARD STERN
NERD AMID LATE TV ...... DAVID LETTERMAN
LIVES .... ELVIS
FRIENDLY JEERS .... JERRY SEINFELD
WOOED ALL NY .... WOODY ALLEN
GENUINE CLASS .... ALEC GUINNESS

One of the most popular word puzzles are anagrams, which are created by rearranging the letters in a word or phrase to spell out something else. The best ones are those that relate to the meaning of the original in some way. Anagrams have been loved for thousands of years. In fact, Louis XIII actually appointed a Royal Anagrammatist to entertain the court with anagrams of people's names! Try your hand at some of these stumpers, and remember, clues to the answers lie in the puzzles themselves!

Riddles: Anagrams

Always be nice to your children because they are the ones who will choose your rest home.

Housework can't kill you, but why take a chance?

I want my children to have all the things I couldn't afford. Then I want to move in with them.

I admit, I have a tremendous sex drive. My boyfriend lives forty miles away.

Whatever you may look like, marry a man your own age—as your beauty fades, so will his eyesight.

What I don't like about office Christmas parties is looking for a job the next day.

I should have suspected my husband was lazy on our wedding day… His mother told me: "I'm not losing a son; I'm gaining a couch."

The last thing my kids ever did to earn money… was lose their baby teeth.

Think of me as a sex symbol for the men who don't give a damn.

Cleaning your house before the kids have stopped growing is like shoveling the walk before it stops snowing.

Phyllis Diller

Sharing stories about her imaginary husband "Fang" and expounding on the hilarity of her life as a housewife and mother, Phyllis Diller's ageless comedy struck a chord with audiences. During her lengthy career, she headlined at nearly every supper club in the U.S. and many more around the world. Known for her overly made-up face and eccentric costumes, Diller got her start when she appeared as a contestant on Groucho Marx's game show You Bet Your Life. *Throughout her career, she has appeared in sixteen movies, acted in countless television specials, and authored five best-selling books, proving that her talents are not only varied, but also timeless.*

Never go to bed mad.
Stay up and fight.

Blonde Quickies

Why did the blonde scale the chain-link fence?

To see what was on the other side.

What did the blonde say when she saw Cheerios?

Oh look, doughnut seeds!

What do you call a brunette with a blonde on either side?

An interpreter.

How can you tell when a blonde has been making chocolate-chip cookies?

You find M&M shells all over the kitchen floor.

Why do blondes like cars with sunroofs?

More legroom.

Why can't a blonde make ice cubes?

She doesn't know the recipe.

Why did the blonde stare at the orange juice container?

It said concentrate.

What is a blonde with brunette dyed hair?

Artificial intelligence.

How can you tell a blonde has been working at your computer?

There is white-out all over the monitor.

How do you make a blonde laugh on Monday?

Tell her a joke on Friday.

How do you get a one-armed blonde out of a tree?

Wave to her.

What goes "vroom-screech, vroom-screech?"

A blonde driving through a flashing red light.

What does a postcard from a blonde's vacation say?

Having a wonderful time. Where am I?

In the Garden of
Eden sat Adam,
Disporting himself
with his madam.
She was filled
with elation,
For in all of creation
There was only
one man—and
she had'm.

Laughable Limericks

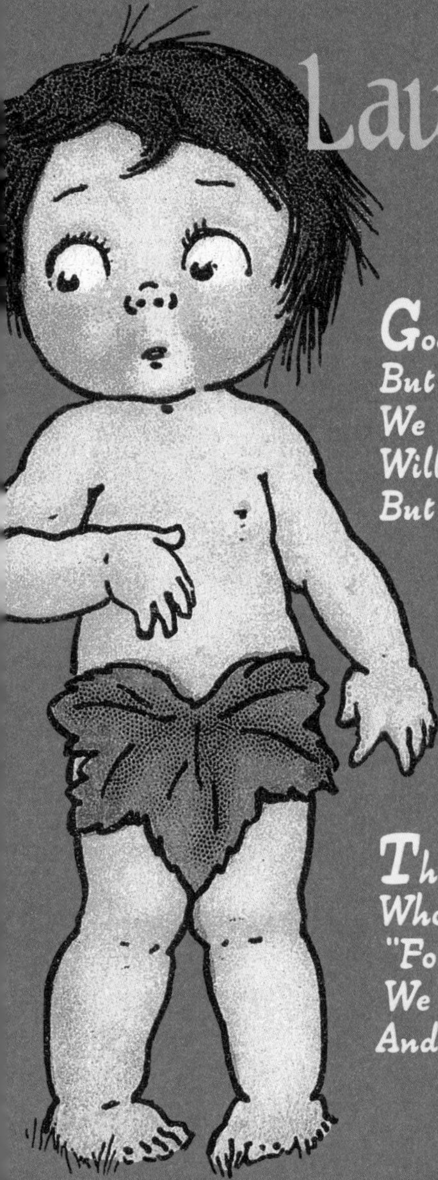

God's plan made a hopeful beginning,
But Man spoilt his chances by sinning;
We trust that the story
Will end in great glory,
But at present the other side's winning

An ardent gravedigger named Quirk
Fell in love with Elizabeth Burke
But on meeting rejection
He curbed his dejection
By throwing himself into his work.

There once was a pious young priest,
Who lived almost wholly on yeast;
"For," he said, "it is plain
We must all rise again,
And I want to get started at least."

A Jewish grandma and her grandson are at the beach. He's playing in the water, she is standing on the shore watching him, when all of a sudden, a huge wave rises up from nowhere and crashes onto the spot where the boy is wading. The water recedes and the boy is nowhere to be seen.

The grandma holds her hands to the sky, screams and cries:

"Lord, how could you? Haven't I been a wonderful grandmother? Haven't I been a wonderful mother? Haven't I kept a kosher home? Haven't I given to charity? Haven't I lit candles every Friday night? Haven't I tried my very best to live a life that you would be proud of?"

A voice booms back from the sky, "All right already!"

A moment later another huge wave rises up out of nowhere and crashes on the beach. As the water recedes, the boy is standing there. He is smiling and splashing around as if nothing had ever happened.

The voice booms again. "I have returned your grandson. Are you satisfied?"

She responds, "He had a hat."

A little boy gets on the bus, sits next to a man reading a book, and notices he has his collar on backwards. The little boy asks why he wears his collar that way.

The man, who is a priest, says, "I am a Father."

The little boy replies, "My father doesn't wear his collar like that."

The priest looks up from his book and answers, "I am the Father of many."

The little boy says, "My dad has four boys, four girls, and two grandchildren, and he doesn't wear his collar that way."

The priest, getting impatient, says, "I am the Father of hundreds," and went back to reading his book.

The little boy sits quietly, but on leaving the bus, leans over and says, "Well, maybe you should wear your pants backwards instead of your collar."

Little Billy was doing very badly in math. His parents had tried everything: tutors, etc; they tried everything they could think of.

Finally, in a last-ditch effort, they took Billy down and enrolled him in the local Catholic school. After the first day, little Billy came home with a very serious look on his face. He didn't even kiss his mother hello. Instead, he went straight to his room and hit the books. His mother was amazed. She called him down to dinner and to her shock, the minute he was done, he marched back to his room without a word and went back to studying. This went on for some time, day after day, without any explanation.

Finally, little Billy brought home his report card. He quietly handed it his mother and went to study. She tore open the envelope and to her amazement, little Billy got an A in math! Now she could no longer hold back her curiosity and went straight to her son's room.

"I must know, what was it? Was it the nuns?" she asked.

Little Billy looked at her and shook his head, no.

"Well, then, was it the books, the discipline, the structure, the uniforms? What was it?"

Little Tommy looked at her and said, "Well, on the first day of school, when I saw that guy nailed to the plus sign, I knew they weren't fooling around."

Tommy O'Connor went to confession and said, "Forgive me Father, for I have sinned." "What have you done, Tommy O'Connor?" asked the priest.

"I had sex with a girl," answered Tommy contritely.

"I see," said the priest. "Who was it, Tommy?"

"I cannot tell you Father, please

forgive me for my sin."

"Was it Mary Margaret Sullivan?" asked the priest.

"No Father, please forgive me for my sin but I cannot tell you who it was," replied Tommy

"Was it Catherine Mary McKenzie?" persisted the priest.

"No Father, please forgive me for my sin," repeated Tommy.

"Well then it has to be Sarah Martha O'Keefe," declared the priest.

"No Father, please forgive me, I cannot tell you who it was."

"Okay, Tommy go say five Hail Mary's and four Our Fathers and you will be abolished of your sin."

So Tommy walked out to the pews where his friend Joseph was waiting.

"What did ya get?" asked Joseph.

"Well I got five Hail Mary's, four Our Fathers, and three good leads."

John and Marie went to the same Baptist church. One Sunday, he was in the pew right behind Marie and he noticed what an attractive woman she was. He decided to ask her out to dinner that weekend, and to his surprise, she agreed.

So on Saturday night, John picked Marie up in his car and took her to the finest restaurant in town. When they sat down, John asked politely, "Would you like a cocktail before dinner?"

"Oh, no, John," replied Marie. "What would I tell my Sunday-school class?"

Well, John was taken aback, but he didn't say anything.

After dinner, he reached into his pocket and pulled out a pack of cigarettes.

"Hey, Marie," said John, "Would you like a smoke?"

"Oh, no, John," said Marie. "What would I tell my Sunday-school class?"

Well, John was feeling pretty low after that, so he decided to drive

Marie home. Along the way they passed the Holiday Inn. He'd struck out twice already, so he figured he had nothing to lose. "Hey, Marie," said John, "how would you like to stop at this motel with me?"

"Sure, John, that would be nice," said Marie.

Well, John couldn't believe his luck. He immediately did a U-turn and drove back to the motel and checked in with Marie.

The next morning John got up first. He looked at Marie lying there in the bed and was suddenly overcome with guilt. He gently shook Marie awake and said, "Marie, I've got to ask you one thing. What are you going to tell your Sunday-school class?"

Marie said, "The same thing I always tell them . . . You don't have to smoke and drink to have a good time."

A very religious Christian woman always carried a Bible when she traveled on a plane. Flying made her extremely nervous, and reading her Bible helped relax her.

One time, the man sitting next to her chuckled a little when he saw her pull out her Bible. After a while, he turned to her and asked, "You don't really believe all that stuff in there do you?"

The lady replied, "Of course I do. It is the Bible."

He said, "Well, what about that guy that was swallowed by that whale?"

She replied, "Oh, Jonah. Yes, I believe that, it is in the Bible."

He asked, "Well, how do you suppose he survived all that time inside the whale?"

The lady said, "Well, I don't

really know. I guess when I get to heaven, I will ask him."

"What if he isn't in heaven?" the man asked sarcastically.

"Then *you* can ask him." replied the lady.

A new young priest at his first mass was so nervous he could hardly speak. After mass, he asked the monsignor how he had done. The monsignor replied, "When I am worried about getting nervous on the pulpit, I put a glass of vodka next to the water glass. If I start to get anxious, I take a sip." So the next Sunday, he took the monsignor's advice. At the beginning of the sermon, he got nervous and took a drink. He proceeded to talk up a storm. Upon his return to his office after mass, he found the following note on his door:

1. Next time, sip the vodka, don't gulp.
2. There are 10 commandments, not 12.
3. There are 12 disciples, not 10.
4. Jesus was consecrated, not constipated.
5. David slew Goliath. He did not kick the shit out of him.
6. We do not refer to Jesus Christ as the late J.C.
7. The Father, Son, and Holy Ghost are not referred to as Daddy, Junior, and the Spook.
8. When David was hit by a rock and knocked off his donkey, do not say he was stoned off his ass.
9. We do not refer to the cross as the "Big T."
10. The recommended way to say grace before a meal is not: Rub-A-Dub-Dub thanks for the grub, yay God.
11. And lastly, the Virgin Mary should never, under any circumstances, be called "Mary with the cherry."

Did you hear about the dyslexic rabbi?

He walks around saying "Yo."

There was a young
parson named Perkins

Exceedingly fond
of small gherkins.

One summer at tea
He ate forty-three,

Which pickled his
internal workins.

FAKE COFFEE SPILL You can purchase ready-made fake coffee spills, but it's so much funnier if you use someone's favorite cup to make it truly believable. Place it near their computer keyboard or some important documents and watch all hell break loose!

Materials: disposable or ceramic coffee mug, white glue, brown puff paint, waxed paper

1. Mix together equal parts white glue and brown puff paint. Adjust the amount of paint until the mixture is lighter than the color of the coffee you want—it will darken as it dries.
2. Set the selected tipped-over cup into about a tablespoon of the mixture on a sheet of waxed paper. Pour another 1 to 2 tablespoons on and in front of the mug's lip or cup's sipping hole. Drying time can be up to a week.
3. Peel off the waxed paper and have fun!

Cup o' Joke

Every night, my wife calls me to dinner in the same way. She yells out, "Dinner's on the table. Come and guess it!"

You can fool some of the people some of the time and some of the people all of the time. That's usually enough. For potential disasters, this pessimist carries a card in his wallet that says, "In case of accident, I'm not surprised." An optimist is a guy who looks forward to the great scenery on a detour. Cockiness is the feeling you have just before you know better. Sin is skating on thin ice and ending up in hot water. Abstinence isn't bad if practiced in moderation! I was so cold last night, it took me an hour to get my girl started! She looks as if she was poured into her dress but forgot to say "when." Medicine is a great profession—you get a

Milton Berle

One of the pioneering legends of television, comedian Milton Berle worked for more than eight decades in show business, both as a brilliant comedian and as an accomplished actor. His acting career started early with numerous silent film roles and vaudeville routines as a child. After honing his craft on the stage, Berle took a chance in the new medium of television, hosting The Texaco Star Theater. *Television perfectly suited his brand of slapstick comedy, and the show was a nationwide hit, attracting huge audiences and major sponsors. In addition to his role as "Mr. Television," Milton Berle appeared in numerous films, and throughout his life mentored many who wanted to get a start in the business.*

woman to take off her clothes and then you send her husband the bill. As Jack the Ripper's mother said to her son, "How come you never go out with the same girl twice?" One fellow felt that his marriage was secure. But a month after he and his wife moved from New York to Kansas City, he discovered that they still had the same mailman. A doctor told a prostitute, "Take these pills, eat a bland diet, and in three days I'll have you back in bed." A union official told his grandson a bedtime story, beginning, "Once upon a time and a half…" My church welcomes all denominations—tens, twenties, fifties… He's so rich, when he buys a suit the tailor has to let out the pockets! She's so ritzy, the bags under her eyes are Gucci! All you get when you pick my pocket is practice. Times are so bad, hitchhikers are offering to go either way! I used to be bullish, then I was bearish. Now I'm brokish! My son was about seven when he looked into our wedding album and said, "Pop, are these pictures of the day Mom came to work for us?" It's amazing. One day you look at your phone bill and realize they're teenagers! I just gave my son a hint. On his room door I put a sign: CHECKOUT TIME IS 18.

Classic Comics

Milton Berle

My wife is so frigid, when she opens her mouth a light goes on! A man took his wife to a psychiatrist and said, "What's-her-name here complains that I don't give her enough attention!" A husband answered the phone, "No, I'm afraid she's not in at the moment. Who shall I say was going to listen?" They're having an age problem. He won't act his, and she won't tell hers. Aging is when you've come a long way, baby, and you just ran out of gas. I must have had a little too much to drink on my birthday. I lit the candles on my cake with one breath! I'm growing old by myself. My wife hasn't had a birthday in ten years! As the cow said to the farmer, "Thanks for the warm hand!"

Love at first sight saves a lot of time.

Vegetable Verse

"Come, lettuce get married," said Arti.
"Will your celery keep two?" asked she.
"With carrot will do and I think, dear,
Something better will turnip," said he.
So off to old Pars'n Ipps cottage
Onion road, the wedding to stage,
They spud, and it took but a second
In this modern taxi-cabbage.
But you can't beet a taxicab meter;
Appeasing the bill left him broke,
Caused a lump to sprout in his thorax
And nearly made poor Artichoke.
However, they weren't cress fallen;
To the house on the corner they went,
Woke the pars'nip up from his slumber,
On the greensward held the event.
And that is the endive my story
For there isn't much room left to write!

Do you carrot all for me, for my heart beets for you, and my Love is as soft as a squash, but as strong as an onion. For you are a peach, with your radish hair and turnip nose. You are the apple of my eye, so if we cantaloupe then lettuce marry, anyhow, for I know we would make a happy pear.

Two carrots are riding together in a car one night. They get into a terrible accident and are both taken to the hospital. One of the carrots just has a few bumps and bruises so he sits in the waiting room to see how his friend is.

After many hours the doctor comes out of the operating room and says to the carrot, "I have good news and bad news–which do you want to here first?"

The carrot said, "The good news, doctor."

So the doctor says, "The good news is that your friend is going to live."

"Well what's the bad news, doctor?" the carrot asked.

"The bad news is that he's going to be a vegetable for the rest of his life."

A wee wee man
in a red coat.
Staff in my hand,
stone in my throat.
What am I?
A Cherry!

For answers see bottom of page 279.

Riddles: What Am I?

1. I cannot be felt, seen or touched; yet I can be found in everybody; my existence is always in debate; yet I have my own style of music. What am I?

2. I can sizzle like bacon, I am made with an egg,
I have plenty of backbone, but lack a good leg,
I peel layers like onions, but still remain whole,
I can be long, like a flagpole, yet fit in a hole,
What am I?

3. You can find me in darkness but never in light.
I am present in daytime but absent at night.
In the deepest of shadows, I hide in plain sight.
What am I?

4. I am the ruler of shovels. I have a double. I am as thin as a knife. I have a wife. What am I?

5. I am a rock group that has four members, all of whom are dead, one of which was assassinated. What am I?

6. I have two arms, but fingers none. I have two feet, but cannot run. I carry well, but I have found I carry best with my feet off the ground. What am I?

7. He has one and a person has two, a citizen has three and a human being has four, a personality has five and an inhabitant of earth has six. What am I?

8. I am used to bat with, yet I never get a hit. I am near a ball, yet it is never thrown. What am I?

9. I start with the letter E, I end with the letter E. I contain only one letter, Yet I am not the letter E! What am I?

10. Round I start, yet no shape have I. Allow me to breathe, and my life will die. The older I grow, the more sought-after I become. You will feel much better when I am done. What am I?

11. I live above a star, but do not burn. I have 11 friends that do not turn. My initials are PRS. What am I?

12. I come in different shapes and sizes. Parts of me are curves, others are straight. You can put me anywhere you like, but there is only one right place for me. What am I?

13. Three-fourths of a cross and a circle complete, two semicircles with a perpendicular meet. Then add a triangle that stands on two feet, two semicircles and a circle complete. What am I?

14. Forward I'm heavy, backward I'm not. What am I?

Answers: **1.** A soul. **2.** A snake. **3.** The letter "D" **4.** The King of Spades. **5.** Mt. Rushmore. **6.** A wheelbarrow. **7.** A syllable. **8.** Eyelashes. **9.** An envelope. **10.** A bottle of wine. **11.** The number 7 on a touch-tone telephone.**12.** A jigsaw puzzle piece. **13.** TOBACCO. **14.** TON.

Consider the poor
hippopotamus:

His life is unduly
monotonous.

He lives
half asleep

At the edge
of the deep,

And his face
is as big as
his bottom is.

Laughable Limericks

It is the unfortunate habit
Of a rabbit to breed like a rabbit.
One can say without question
This leads to congestion
In the burrows that rabbits inhabit.

Ferrets live by a code tried and true,
From which humans can benefit too:
Teach your sons and daughters
To do unto otters,
As otters would do unto you.

Oh, a wondrous bird is the Pelican.
His beak can hold more than his belican.
He can hold in his beak
Enough food for a week!
But I'll be darned if I know how the helican.

—Dixon Lanier Merritt

Why did the parrot wear a raincoat?
Because she wanted to be Polly unsaturated!

Animal One-liners

What do you call a woodpecker with no beak?
A headbanger.

What did the cat say when he lost all his money?
I'm paw.

What's worse than raining cats and dogs?
Hailing taxicabs!

What do you call an elephant who can't add?
Dumbo.

Why did the cat frown when she passed the henhouse?
Because she heard fowl language.

What did one flea say to the other?
"Shall we walk, or take the dog?"

What did the grape say when the elephant stood on it?
Nothing, it just let out a little wine.

Why did the ram fall off the cliff?
He didn't see the ewe turn.

What do you call two elephants on a bicycle?
Optimistic.

What kind of bees make milk?
Boobies!

How can you tell when there's an elephant under the bed?
When you sit and hit your head on the ceiling.

What do you call a pig who loses his voice?
Disgruntled.

A Woman and a Parrot

A woman was thinking about buying a family pet and decided she wanted a beautiful parrot. It wouldn't be as much work as a dog, and it would be fun to hear it speak.

She went to a pet shop and immediately spotted a large, beautiful parrot. There was a sign on the cage that said $50.

"Why so little?" she asked the pet store owner.

The owner looked at her and said, "Look, I should tell you first that this bird used to live in a raunchy whorehouse and sometimes it says some pretty vulgar stuff."

The woman thought about this awhile, but decided she had to have the bird anyway. She took it home and hung the bird's cage up in her living room and waited for it to say something.

The bird looked around the room a little, then at her, and said, "New house, new madam."

The woman was a bit shocked at this implication, but then thought, "That's not so bad."

When her two teenage daughters returned from school, the bird saw them and said, "New house, new madam, new whores."

The girls and the woman were a bit offended, but then began to laugh about the whole situation.

Moments later, the woman's husband came home from work. The bird looked right at him and said, "Hi Keith!"

A Letter from John Cheever to Joesphine Herbst

In 1961, John Cheever and his family took in a cat belonging to their friend, Josephine Herbst. Cheever and the feline, named Delmore, became mortal enemies at once. After living with Delmore for nearly two years, Cheever put pen to paper to write Herbst an update on her former cat's well-being.

Cedar lane
Ossining
Some Friday

Dear Josie,
It's been years since we had anything but the most sketchy communications....I've long since owed you an account of the destiny of your cat and here we go.

The cat, after your leaving him, seemed not certain of his character or his place and we changed his name to Delmore which immediately made him more vivid. The first sign of his vividness came when he dumped a load in a Kleenex box while I was suffering from a cold. During a paroxysm of sneezing I grabbed for some kleenex. I shall not overlook my own failures in this tale but when I got the cat shit off my face and the ceiling I took Delmore to the kitchen door and drop-kicked him into the

clothesyard. This was an intolerable cruelty and I have not yet been forgiven. He is not a forgiving cat. Indeed he is proud. Spring came on then and as I was about to remove the clear glass storm window from Fred's room, Delmore, thinking the window to be open, hurled himself against the glass. This hurt his nose and his psyche badly. Mary and the children then went to the Mountains and I spent a reasonably happy summer cooking for Delmore. The next eventfulness came on Thanksgiving. When the family had gathered for dinner and I was about to carve the turkey there came a strangling noise from the bathroom. I ran there and found Delmore sitting in the toilet, neck-deep in cold water and very sore. I got him out and dried him with towels but there was no forgiveness. Shortly after Christmas a Hollywood writer and his wife came to lunch. My usual salutation to Delmore is: Up yours, and when the lady heard me say this she scorned me and gathered Delmore to her breasts. Delmore, in a flash, started to unscrew her right eyeball and the lady, trying to separate herself from Delmore lost a big pieces of an Italian dress she was wearing which Mary said cost $250.00. This was not held against Delmore and a few days later when we had a skating party I urged Delmore to come to the pond with us. He seemed pleased and frisked along like a family-loving cat but at that moment a little wind came from the north-east and spilled the snow off a hemlock onto Delmore, he gave me a dirty look, went back to the house and dumped another load into the kleenex box. This time he got the cleaning-woman and they remain unfriendly.

This is not meant at all to be a rancorous account and I think Delmore enjoys himself. I have been accused of cruelty and a woman named Ruth Hershberger keeps writing Elizabeth Pollet, telling her to take the cat away from me, but Delmore contributes a dynamic to all our relationships. People who dislike me go directly to his side and he is, thus, a peace-maker. He loves to play with toilet paper. He does not like catnip mice. He does not kill song birds. In the spring the rabbits chase him around the lawn but they leave after the lettuce has been eaten and he has the terrace pretty much to himself. He is very fat these days and his step, Carl Sandburg not withstanding, sounds more like that of a barefoot middle-aged man on his way to the toilet than the settling in of a winter fog but he has his role and we all respect it and here endeth my report on Delmore the cat.

I hope all is well with you. Mary teaches, I write, the children go to various schools and all is well.

Best,
John

The Crocodile's Toothache
By Shel Silverstein

The Crocodile
Went to the dentist
And sat down in the chair,
And the dentist said, "Now tell me, sir,
Why does it hurt and where?"
And the Crocodile said, "I'll tell you the truth,
I have a terrible ache in my tooth,"
And he opened his jaws so wide, so wide,
That the dentist, he climbed right inside,
And the dentist laughed, "Oh isn't this fun?"
As he pulled the teeth out, one by one.
And the Crocodile cried, "You're hurting me so!
Please put down your pliers and let me go."
But the dentist just laughed with a Ho Ho Ho,
And he said, "I still have twelve to go–
Oops, that's the wrong one, I confess,
But what's one crocodile's tooth, more or less?"
Then suddenly, the jaws went SNAP,
And the dentist was gone, right off the map,
And where he went one could only guess . . .
To North or South or East or West . . .
He left no forwarding address.
But what's one dentist, more or less?

What do you get if you cross a compass and a shellfish?

A guided mussel.

What do you get when you cross...

What do you get if you cross an owl with a goat?

A hootenanny.

What do you get if you cross a sports reporter with a vegetable?

A common tater!

What do you get if you cross an artist with a policeman?

A brush with the law!

What do you get if you cross a tortoise and a storm?

An "I'm not in a hurry cane."

What do you get if you cross a cow with a crystal ball?

A message from the udder side.

What do you get if you cross an insomniac, an agnostic, and a dyslexic?

Someone who lies awake all night long wondering if there really is a dog.

What do you get if you cross a frog with a traffic warden?

Toad away.

What do you get when you cross a cocker spaniel, a poodle and a ghost?

Cockapoodleboo!

What do you get if you cross an impressionist painter and a New York City cabdriver?

*Vincent Van Go F**k Yourself!*

OFFIC
NOVEL
CANDY

FOOLISH QUESTIONS

Milton Berle

I'm the president of the Society for the Prevention of Foolish Questions. We're only a small group at present, but give us time and we'll put an end to your getting a phone call at three in the morning and the voice at the other end asking, "Did I wake you?" No, you moron! I had to get up to answer the phone. When you bring a young lady some flowers and candy, she asks, "For me?" No, for your dog! Then there's the beauty where you're walking across the street, get dusted by a car, fall to the ground in a heap, and the driver calls back, "Did I hurt you?" Of course not! I always bleed when I walk! The foolish questions asked by various people where a would-be speaker works provide great sport for part of a humorous speech. You can get big laughs by mentioning by name any dummy who always walks over to a secretary typing away with ninety fingers and asks, "Are you through yet?" My internist had a receptionist who always asked, "Are you here to see the doctor?" No, I want to fool around with a nurse!

PRANK CALLS

Revisit one of the naughty pleasures of childhood and try out some of these harmless prank calls next time you want to play a joke on a friend or family member. Just make sure your victim has a good sense of humor!

"Hi, I'm looking for . . ."

Amanda Huggenkiss
Anna Dapter
Avery Niceman
Jenna Rossity
Orson Cart
Polly Eurathane
Jean-Ann Tonique
Lucy Lastik
Earl E. Bird
Jim Nassium
Drew P. Draughers

"Hello, do you know . . ."

Ivana Tinkle
Mike Rotch
Nick Roffillia
I.P. Freely
Anita Bath

"Hello, I'd like . . ."

Oliver Kloushoff
Neil Downe
Herb Altey
Chris P. Duck
Ann Chovy
Les Hair

"Hi, is there a . . . in the house?

Tish Shue
Matt Ress
Hugh Jass
Dora Jarre
Crystal Chandra Lear
Al Coholic
Anna Rexic
Jacques Strap
Jim Pansey
Claire Voyant

"Excuse me, are you . . ."

Wanda Phull
A. Stu Pidass
Joe King
Holden Magroin
Gladys Friday
Fran Tick

The audience was large and respectable. One man was large and the other was respectable.

I'm so mad I could chew the paper pants off a lamb chop. He isn't cheap; he just has low pockets and short arms. I learned to rumba very early in life… I had a tricycle with a loose seat. The landlord was generous. He gave me wall-to-wall floors. "Did you say that Elizabeth Taylor is writing a book?" "Yes… It goes Chap one, Chap two, Chap three… " A drunk went up to a telephone pole and felt his way all around it. "Good Lord!" he cried, "I'm walled in!" A guy has just invented a device to cut down on unnecessary noise inside an automobile. It fits right over her mouth. HE: It's to be a battle of wits. SHE: How brave of you to go unarmed. There's a method for going back home from Las Vegas with a small fortune. Go there with a large fortune. A truthful woman is one who doesn't lie about anything except her age, weight, and her husband's salary. Marriage begins when he sinks in your arms and it ends with your arms in the sink. Adam had no mother-in-law. That's why he called it Paradise. He got to walking in his sleep so much we finally had to tattoo some underwear on him. I never swear on Sunday—but tomorrow you can all go to hell. Wherever there's smoke, there's toast. Our idea of a skeptic is a man who sees twenty people waiting for the elevator and then goes up and pushes the button. The human brain is a wonderful thing. It starts working the moment you are born, and never stops until you stand up to speak in public.

Steve Allen

Though many know Steve Allen from his successes in television, this comedian, actor, composer, and author was truly a Renaissance man. Born to the vaudevillian comedy team of Montrose and Allen, Steve started his career in radio and appeared on numerous game and talk shows. His wisecracking persona and quick wit made him the perfect host for NBC's newest variety program, The Tonight Show. *Reaching the peak of his fame in the 1960s with* The Steve Allen Show *and* The Steve Allen Comedy Hour, *Allen continued working into the 1990s composing thousands of songs, appearing in films, and writing more than fifty books.*

Kingly Comics

A Brief History of the Court Jester

"Foolery, sir, does walk about the orb like the sun, it shines everywhere." So wrote William Shakespeare in *Twelfth Night*. Although China, India, and Africa have histories of court jesters, people are probably most familiar with the motley-wearing professional fool of medieval Europe.

A buffoon whose main job was to entertain, the jester who was lucky enough to serve the king or queen's court was actually bright, well-traveled, and highly skilled. If want ads had been around back then, one for a jester might have read:

> *Wanted: Agile dwarf, hunchback, or gangly-legged oddball to perform antics, play jokes, sing, eat fire, turn cartwheels, and lift the all-powerful monarch out of melancholy moods; paper folding and ability to create topical rhymes a plus; must be quick-witted but of low social status, so as not to threaten the powers that be, and must be amenable to acting as scapegoat (which could involve beheading) if the situation should arise. Floppy three-pointed hat with jingle bells supplied. Bring your own stilts.*

Beyond the tumbling, laughing jokester we think of, the court jester sometimes played the important role of critic and advisor at court. Acting under the guise of fool and unconstrained by society's laws, he actually had almost a free pass to say what he wanted. Because his words could be taken in jest, the king would not lose face.

With roots reaching back to the comic actors of ancient Rome, court jesters—who first appeared in European courts around 1200 and remained popular for about 400 years—can be seen as the forefathers of today's standup comics.

REAL Funny

PRESIDENTIAL BLOOPERS

Actual statements made by various United States presidents

"Things are more like they are now than they ever were before."
— PRESIDENT DWIGHT D. EISENHOWER

"When the president does it, that means that it is not illegal."
— PRESIDENT RICHARD NIXON

"I have orders to be awakened at any time in the case of a national emergency, even if I'm in a cabinet meeting."
— PRESIDENT RONALD REAGAN

"I never drink coffee at lunch. I find it keeps me awake for the afternoon."
— PRESIDENT RONALD REAGAN

"Now, like, I'm president. It would be pretty hard for some drug guy to come into the White House and start offering it up, you know?... I bet if they did, I hope I would say, 'Hey, get lost. We don't want any of that.'"
— PRESIDENT GEORGE BUSH, SR., SPEAKING TO A GROUP OF STUDENTS ABOUT DRUG ABUSE

"It depends on what the meaning of the word *is* is."
— PRESIDENT BILL CLINTON

"Rarely is the question asked: Is our children learning?"
— PRESIDENT GEORGE W. BUSH

"It's clearly a budget. It's got a lot of numbers in it."
— PRESIDENT GEORGE W. BUSH

"The best way to relieve families from time to time is to let them keep some of their own money."
— PRESIDENT GEORGE W. BUSH

"One of the great things about books is sometimes there are some fantastic pictures."
— PRESIDENT GEORGE W. BUSH

"Nobody needs to tell me what I believe. But I do need somebody to tell me where Kosovo is."
— PRESIDENT GEORGE W. BUSH

"I'm the master of low expectations."
— PRESIDENT GEORGE W. BUSH

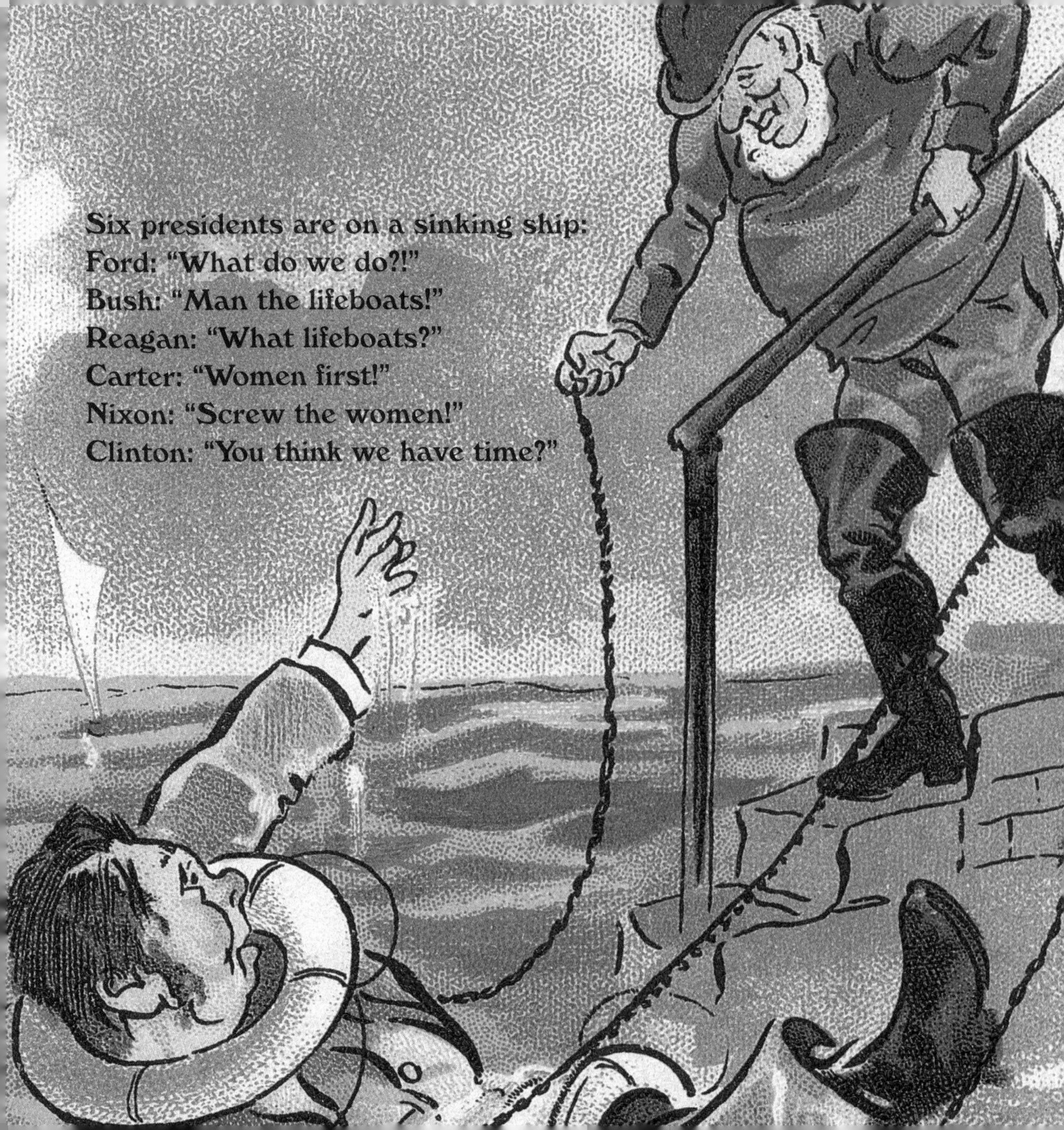
Six presidents are on a sinking ship:
Ford: "What do we do?!"
Bush: "Man the lifeboats!"
Reagan: "What lifeboats?"
Carter: "Women first!"
Nixon: "Screw the women!"
Clinton: "You think we have time?"

First Man: "Have you heard the latest joke about the White House?"

Second Man: "I happen to work in the White House."

First Man: "That's all right. I'll tell it slowly!"

Everywhere you look, there are signs saying, "Washington slept here." No wonder he's the father of our country!

A politician awoke in a hospital bed after a complicated operation and found that the curtains were drawn around him.

"Why are the curtains closed?" he asked. "Is it night?"

A nurse replied, "No, it is just that there is a fire across the street, and we didn't want you waking up and thinking that the operation was unsuccessful."

A brain surgeon was about to perform a brain transplant. "You have your choice of two brains," he told the patient. "For $1000 you can have the brain of a psychologist, or for $10,000 you can have the brain of a politician."

The patient was amazed at the huge price difference. "Is the brain of a politician that much better?" he asked.

The brain surgeon replied, "No, it's not better, just unused."

The president was awakened one night by an urgent call from the Pentagon.

"Mr. President," said the four-star general, barely able to contain himself, "there's good news and bad news."

"Oh no," muttered the President. "Well, let me have the bad news first."

"The bad news, sir, is that we've been invaded by creatures from another planet."

"Gosh, and the good news?"

"The good news, sir, is that they eat reporters and pee oil."

A bachelor is a guy who is footloose and fiancé-free.

A boiled egg in the morning is hard to beat.

He drove his expensive car into a tree
and found out how the Mercedes bends.

It was an emotional wedding.
Even the cake was in tiers.

Those who jump off a Paris bridge are in Seine.

There was once a cross-eyed teacher
who couldn't control his pupils.

The guy who invented the doorknocker got a No-bell prize.

Atheism is a non-prophet organization.

I fired my masseuse today. She just
rubbed me the wrong way.

A Freudian slip is when you say one
thing but mean your mother.

A man needs a mistress just
to break the monogamy.

Alimony is the high cost of leaving.

Marathon
runners
with bad
footwear
suffer the
agony of
da feet.
307

Classic Comics

I always wanted to be somebody, but now I realize I should have been more specific. **I worry that the person who thought up Muzak may be thinking up something else.** If love is the answer, could you please rephrase the question? **Truth is, I've always been selling out. The difference is that in the past, I looked like I had integrity because there were no buyers.** I'm glad I've got delusions of grandeur. It makes me feel a lot better about myself. **Reality is a crutch for people who can't cope with drugs.** Sometimes I worry about being a success in a mediocre world. **Man invented language to satisfy his deep need to complain.** Being a New Yorker is never having to say you're sorry. **Why is it when we talk to God we're said to be praying, but when God talks to us we're schizophrenic?**

Lily Tomlin

Comedienne and actress Lily Tomlin got her first big break portraying the hilarious Edith Ann and Ernestine on the hit TV show Laugh-In *in 1969. She followed up her television career with several films, including* Nashville *(which earned her an Oscar nomination),* Nine to Five, The Incredible Shrinking Woman *and* All of Me. *Her one-woman Broadway show* The Search for Intelligent Life in the Universe *was touted by fans to be Tomlin at her funniest and garnered rave reviews.*

No matter how cynical you become, it's never enough to keep up. **Reality is nothing but a collective hunch.** Ninety-eight percent of the adults in this country are decent, hard-working Americans. It's the other two percent that gets all the publicity. But then, we elected them.

Top Ten Driving Haikus

10. Blink Blink Blink Blink Blink
    Blink Blink Blink Blink Blink Blink Blink.
    Someday, you'll turn left.

9. I'm in a hurry.
   You are driving too slowly.
   I must gesture now.

8. It's always the same:
   "Next exit 84 miles"
   When I have to pee.

7. Run, pedestrian!
   I can't stop! Jump that curb!... Damn.
   Bumpers are *not* cheap.

6. Rearview mirror shows
   Highway patrol behind me.
   How many did I have?

5. Ponytailed boomer
   Doing thirty while singing
   "Life in the Fast Lane."

4. Use the crosswalk, fool!
   I might not react in time!
   Well, those are the brakes.

3. Cut *me* off, you scum?
   Pass you on the right! I win!!
   Morning, officer.

2. Something just happened
   Between me and the leather.
   Please crack a window.

1. My toll-booth hottie
   Can't hear my smooth pickup lines
   Over the car horns.

"I was thrown from my car
as it left the road. I was
later found in a ditch by
some stray cows."

REAL Funny

ACCIDENT REPORTS

Real excerpts from auto-accident insurance claim forms

"A pedestrian hit me and went under my car."

"Coming home, I drove into the wrong house and collided with a tree I don't have."

"No one was to blame for the accident, but it never would have happened if the other driver had been alert."

"The pedestrian had no idea which direction to go, so I ran over him."

"I saw the slow-moving, sad-faced old gentleman as he bounced off the hood of my car."

"I was taking my canary to the hospital. It got loose in the car and flew out the window. The next thing I saw was his rear end, and there was a crash."

"I had been shopping for plants all day and was on my way home. As I reached an intersection, a hedge sprung up, obscuring my vision."

"To avoid hitting the bumper of the car in front, I struck the pedestrian."

"When I could not avoid a collision, I stepped on the gas and crashed into the other car."

"In my attempt to kill a fly, I drove into a telephone pole."

"As I approached the intersection, a stop sign suddenly appeared in a place where no stop sign had ever appeared before. I was unable to stop in time to avoid the accident."

"The guy was all over the road. I had to swerve a number of times before I hit him."

"An invisible car came out of nowhere, struck my vehicle, and vanished."

Classic Comics

There's a fine line between fishing and just standing on the shore like an idiot. **All those who believe in telekinesis, raise my hand.** Ever notice how irons have a setting for "permanent" press? I don't get it… **Anywhere is walking distance if you've got the time.** I have an existential map. It has "You are here" written all over it. **If a word in the dictionary were misspelled, how would we know?** I went to a general store. They wouldn't let me buy anything specifically. **I bought some batteries, but they weren't included.** Last week the candle factory burned down. Everyone just stood around and sang "Happy Birthday." **I used to work at a fire hydrant factory. You couldn't park anywhere near the place.** A clear conscience is usually the sign of a bad memory. **Hermits have no peer pressure.** Doesn't matter what temperature a room is, it's always room temperature.

Steven Wright

With his deadpan delivery, legendary comic Steven Wright made a name for himself through his monotone commentary on the mundane absurdities of life. Starting out in the comedy clubs of Boston in the 1970s, Wright got his big break in 1982 on The Tonight Show *and went on to have numerous television specials over the next twenty years. Wright has played a variety of small movie roles and won an Oscar in 1988 for the short film,* The Appointments of Dennis Jennings, *which he starred in, co-produced, and co-wrote. Fans of Steven Wright can still find him performing his hilariously droll act to sold-out crowds across the country.*

Classic Comics

One time I went through a stop sign and the police stopped me and asked, "Why'd you go through the sign?" And I said, "Hey I don't believe everything I read." I intend to live forever. So far, so good. Imagine if birds were tickled by feathers. You'd see a flock of birds come by laughing. I bought an ant farm. I don't know where I'm gonna find a tractor that small. I was sad because I had no shoes, until I met a man with no feet. So I said, "Got any shoes you're not using?" You can't have everything; where would you put it? If Barbie is so popular, why do you have to buy her friends? I saw this guy hitch-hiking with a sign that said "Heaven." So I hit him.

PG 10

I drive way too fast to worry about cholesterol.

Riddles: Numbers

1. I am a six-digit number.
I am between 400,000 and 499,999.
The sum of all my numbers equals 30.
I have all even numbers.
My thousands digit and my ones digit are the same.
I do not have any O's.
My tens thousands digit and my 10s digit are the same.
My 100-thousands digit and my hundreds digits are different.
What number could I be?

2. What happened in the middle of the twentieth century that will not happen again for 4,000 years?

3. Which is correct: 9 and 5 is 13 OR 9 and 5 are 13?

4. How can you make the following equation true by drawing only one straight line? 5+5+5=550

5. How can half of 12 be 7?

6. The following number is the only one of its kind: 8,549,176,320. Can you figure what is so special about it?

7. What row of numbers comes next?

1
11
21
1211
111221
312211
13112221

Answers: **1.** 428,628. **2.** The year 1961. It reads the same upside down. This will not happen again until the year 6009. **3.** Neither. 9 and 5 equals 14! **4.** Draw a line on the first plus sign to turn it into a 4!—The equation then becomes true. **5.** Slice the top half of the Roman numerals for the number 12—XII—and you get the Roman numerals for the number 7—VII. **6.** It's the only number that has all the digits arranged in alphabetical order. **7.** The next row is: 1113213211. Starting with the second line, every line describes the line before it. In writing, it is: One One; Two Ones; One Two, One One; etc.

Knock, knock.
Who's there?
Luck.
Luck who?
Luck through
the keyhole
and you'll
find out!

Knock, knock. Jokes

Knock, knock.
  Who's there?
Isabel.
  Isabel who?
Isabel not working?

Knock, knock.
  Who's there?
Doris.
  Doris who?
Doris locked—that's why I knocked!

Knock, knock.
  Who's there?
Old lady.
  Old lady who?
I didn't know you could yodel!

Knock, knock.
  Who's there?
Ivan
  Ivan who?
Ivan to suck your blood.

Knock, knock.
  Who's there?
Hitch.
  Hitch who?
Bless you!

Knock, knock.
  Who's there?
Harry, Butch, and Jimmy.
  Harry, Butch, and Jimmy who?
Harry up, Butch your arms around me, and Jimmy a kiss.

Knock, knock.
  Who's there?
Frankfurter.
  Frankfurter who?
Frankfurter lovely evening.

Knock, knock.
  Who's there?
Euripides.
  Euripides who?
Euripides pants, you pay for dese pants.

Knock, knock.
  Who's there?
Police.
  Police who?
Police stop telling these awful Knock Knock jokes.

Said old Peeping
Tom of Fort Lee:

"Peeping ain't what
it's cracked up to be;

I lose all my sleep,

And I peep and
I peep...

And I find 'em all
peeping at me!"

—Morris Bishop

Laughable Limericks

Said an envious, erudite ermine,
"There's one thing I cannot determine:
When a girl wears my coat,
She's a person of note.
When I wear it, I'm called only vermin."

Said the potentate gross and despotic,
"My tastes are more rich than exotic.
I've always adored
Making love in a Ford
Because I'm so auto-erotic."

Said Oedipus Rex, growing red,
"Those head-shrinkers! Would they were dead!
They make such a pother
Because I love mother.
Well, should I love father instead!"
—J. A. Leventhal

Any time four New Yorkers get into a cab together without arguing, a bank robbery has just taken place. Democracy means that anyone can grow up to be president, and anyone who doesn't grow up can be vice president. **If life was fair, Elvis would be alive and all the impersonators would be dead.** The worst gift is a fruitcake. There is only one fruitcake in the entire world, and people keep sending it to each other. **If God didn't want man to hunt, he wouldn't have given us plaid shirts.** When turkeys mate they think of swans. **The difference between divorce and legal separation is that a legal separation gives a husband time to hide his money.** If airline travel is so safe, how come the flight attendants sit right next to the emergency exits? **Happiness is seeing the muscular lifeguard all the girls were admiring leave the beach hand in hand with another muscular lifeguard.** What's all this fuss about plutonium? How could something named after a Disney character be dangerous?

Johnny Carson

Comedian and consummate late-night talk show host, Johnny Carson was a television institution on The Tonight Show *for thirty years. With his natty style and acerbic wit, he became an American icon. Consistently at the top of the ratings, his breezy, relaxed manner, comic monologue, and selection of guests made him an audience favorite. His mastery of the talk show format made him the standard-bearer for hosts to come, inspiring comic greats Jay Leno and David Letterman.*

I was so naive as a kid I used
to sneak behind the barn
and do nothing.

The Best Laughs
on Television

Most of these classic sitcoms and variety shows are no longer airing new episodes, but you can still find plenty of reruns with a little sleuthing and a satellite dish! Or try your local video store for "best of" compilations, and settle onto the sofa for a lazy

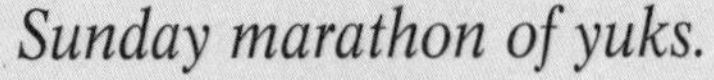
Sunday marathon of yuks.

The Best Laughs on Television

The Abbott and Costello Show (1952) The timeless comedy of Abbott and Costello has resonated for fifty years, with fans still wondering, "Who's on First?"

All in the Family (1971) He may have been a sexist, racist, all-around curmudgeon, but as the man we loved to hate, Archie Bunker delivered the laughs without fail.

The Beverly Hillbillies (1962) You can take a man out of the hills, but you can't take the hillbilly out of a man. The Clampetts brought the country to good ol' Californy and kept their fans entertained with a hilarious brand of slapstick.

The Bob Newhart Show (1972) For nearly six years, psychologist Bob Hartley's daft sense of humor and buttoned-down persona kept his depressed and neurotic patients out of the nuthouse and his audience in stitches.

The Carol Burnett Show (1967) If Carol Burnett hadn't been a comedian, actress, or singer, she might have been misdiagnosed with multiple personality disorder. With her talented cast, this hilarious variety show marked itself as one of a dying breed.

Cheers (1982) Who needs to visit the bar when it can be delivered into your living room? Every viewer felt like they were just one of the gang as Sam, Cliff, Coach, Diane, Carla, and "Norm!" enjoyed a relaxing beer after work… or before work… or during work…

The Cosby Show (1984) Dr. Cliff Huxtable and his attorney wife Claire headed up one of TV's most beloved sitcom families. The show's enormous popularity was due mainly to star Bill Cosby's understated yet goofy brand of humor.

The Dick Van Dyke Show (1961) In this classic family sitcom co-starring Mary Tyler Moore, Dick Van Dyke plays a husband and comedy show writer at the mercy of its egotistical star. The series offered a hilarious glimpse into the work and home life of a modern young married couple.

The Honeymooners (1955) Starring the comedic talents of Jackie Gleason as the hot-headed loudmouth Ralph Kramden and Art Carney as his unflappable sidekick, this show's timeless slapstick humor still cracks up audiences today.

I Love Lucy (1951) This ageless TV standard flaunts Lucille Ball's exaggerated mishaps and riotous exploits with her Cuban bandleader husband, Ricky, and their neighbors Fred and Ethel. The mother of all sitcoms.

The Jeffersons (1975) Nasty, cranky and loud. No, it's not another description for Archie Bunker, although George Jefferson resembled him greatly. Audiences couldn't resist tuning in every week to watch George throw around his insults while wife "Weezy" kept him in line.

The Milton Berle Show (1948) "Mr. Television" can be credited with the exponential increase in the sale of television sets during the early 1950s—all the "ladies and germs" were clamoring to see Uncle Miltie's outrageous variety show.

Monty Python's Flying Circus (1969) This group of English comedians parlayed their decidedly British sense of humor into a cutting-edge series that produced classic sketches like "The Ministry of Silly Walks," "Fish-slapping Dance," and "The Dead Parrot."

Mork & Mindy (1978) A wacky sitcom that tells the continuing story of an alien sent to Earth to observe its creatures, *Mork & Mindy* was a showcase for Robin Williams's brilliant ad-lib humor and wild comic antics.

Red Skelton Show (1951) If Red didn't win your laughter with crazy characters like Junior the Mean Widdle Kid or the drunkard Willy Lump-Lump, he stole it by purposely falling into the orchestra pit.

Roseanne (1988) Roseanne's trailer-park humor and acid-tongued retorts filled prime time with a family-size portion of comic entertainment.

Saturday Night Live (1975) From "Buckwheat Sings" to "Wayne's World," SNL has embedded itself in the American psyche and has given us such premier comedians as John Belushi, Eddie Murphy, Dan Akroyd, and Adam Sandler.

Seinfeld (1990) Between Jerry's ruminations on the minutiae of everyday life, George's penny-pinching, Kramer's wacky schemes, and Elaine's string of failed relationships, this crew created an awful lot of laughter out of "nothing."

The Simpsons (1989) This bumbling family from Springfield, U.S.A. features the hijinks of wisecracking Bart, his smarty-pants vegetarian sister Lisa, and the beer-guzzling antics of their half-wit dad, Homer. Peppered with *au courant* political humor and witty repartee, this is no kiddy cartoon.

Taxi (1978) The ensemble cast, including Christopher Lloyd's Reverend Jim, Andy Kauffman's Latka Gravas, and Danny DeVito's despotic Louis Depalma, gave this smartly written blue-collar comedy an authentic New York feel.

The Tonight Show starring Johnny Carson (1962) "Heeeeeeeere's Johnny!" Ed McMahon's ubiquitous announcement heralded Carson's arrival for more than 4,500 hilarious episodes. Classic comic sketches and Johnny's signature golf swing made him a favorite in homes all over America.

Three's Company (1977) For seven years audiences tuned in to "where the kisses are hers and hers and his" to see how clumsy Jack Tripper, naive Chrissy, and girl-next-door Janet would get out of yet another classic misunderstanding.

Your Show of Shows (1950) This classic variety show featured the comedic talents of Sid Caesar, Imogene Coca, and Carl Reiner, and kicked off the writing careers of comic legends Mel Brooks, Neil Simon and Woody Allen.

How many blondes
does it
take to
change a
light bulb?
One. She just stands there holding
the bulb while the whole world
revolves around her.

Lightbulb Jokes

How many men does it take to screw in a lightbulb?

Three. One to screw in the bulb, and two to listen to him brag about the screwing part.

How many psychiatrists does it take to screw in a lightbulb?

Just one, but the lightbulb has to want to change.

How many grad students does it take to change a lightbulb?

One, but it takes ten years.

How many mice does it take to screw in a lightbulb?

Two. The trick is getting them in there.

How many IRS agents does it take to screw in a lightbulb?

Only one, but it really gets screwed.

How many accountants does it take to screw in a lightbulb?

What kind of answer did you have in mind?

How many civil servants does it take to change a lightbulb?

45: One to change the bulb, and 44 to do the paperwork.

How many surreal-ists does it take to screw in a lightbulb?

Two. One to hold the giraffe and one to put the clocks in the bathtub.

How many telemarketers does it take to change a lightbulb?

Only one, but she has to do it while you're eating dinner.

"Not to be used as protection from a tornado."

—On a blanket from Taiwan

REAL Funny

PRODUCT LABELS

Actual label instructions on consumer goods from around the world

"Remember, objects in the mirror are actually behind you."

—On a helmet-mounted mirror used by cyclists

"Keep out of children."

—On a Korean kitchen knife

"Do not use for drying pets."

—In the manual for a microwave oven

"For use by trained personnel only."

—On a can of air freshener

"Do not use intimately."

—On a tube of deodorant

"Warning: Never iron clothes on the body."

—On an Australian iron

"Caution: The contents of this bottle should not be fed to fish."

—On a bottle of shampoo for dogs

"Recycled flush water unsafe for drinking."

—On a toilet at a public sports facility in Ann Arbor, Michigan

"Warning: Has been found to cause cancer in laboratory mice."

—On a box of rat poison

"Caution: Remove infant before folding for storage."

—On a portable stroller

"Wearing of this garment does not enable you to fly."

—On a child-size Superman costume

"Warning: May contain nuts."

—On a package of peanuts

"Remove wrapper, open mouth, insert muffin, eat."

—On the packaging for a muffin

"Caution: You must remove clothes before washing."

—In a washing machine manual

There was an old
person of Brill,

Who purchased a
shirt with a frill;

But they said,
"Don't you wish

You mayn't look
like a fish,

You obsequious Old
Person of Brill?"

—Edward Lear

Laughable Limericks

A macho young swimmer named Dwyer,
Really liked playing with fire.
One night in the dark
He swam with a shark,
And his voice is now two octaves higher.

An elderly man called Keith
Mislaid his set of false teeth—
They'd been laid on a chair,
He'd forgot they were there,
Sat down, and was bitten beneath.

A gourmet dining at Crewe
Found a rather large mouse in his stew.
Said the waiter, "Don't shout
And wave it about,
Or the rest will be wanting one, too."

GOING BALD

Dennis Miller

Now, I don't want to get off on a rant here, but in our culture, there is no greater cause of agony, insecurity, or Porsche 911 sales than baldness.

What genetic squirting flower is it that determines which of us ends up looking like Robert Plant and which of us ends up looking like Mel Cooley?

Come on, guys, you know how it works. One day you are standing in front of a mirror with a full head of hair and the next you're trying to get the "most coverage" out of the few hairs you have left, like the guy spreading crushed gravel on your driveway.

There are certain telltale signs that you might be losing your hair that you should be aware of.

If you find yourself actually wondering what baseball cap is appropriate for a funeral.

If you notice your barber just making the clicking noise with the scissors without actually touching your hair.

And if your nickname at work is "D**khead" and you're a nice guy.

Entire careers have been built on having hair. I'll say it right now. Had I been bald, I never would have gotten this far in show business. I would have had to write for somebody with hair. In fact, that's really what separates the performers from the writers in Hollywood—hair. My entire writing staff is completely hairless. They hate me. But I don't care because they're a bunch of pathetic, bald losers.

But I realize my head gravy days are numbered. The once-bustling downtown of my abundantly populated scalp is becoming a wasteland of burned-out storefronts and boarded-up windows as the occupants move to the outlying suburbs of my neck, ears and back.

You can try to compensate for your loss in other areas, but the truth is no amount of money or fame will change the fact that you look like the guy who takes the youth group to sing at the nursing home.

When you think about it, hair is all we men have got. We don't have the option of using makeup to hide the flaws in our appearance or enhance our good traits. Once the hair goes, that's it. And then we're faced with the distasteful task of having to cultivate other attributes to make ourselves attractive. And frankly, who's got the time? I mean, I've got a wife, two kids, and golf. My dance card's full enough without my having to go out and get a f**king personality. Okay?

Now, there are many different ways to soften the blow of nature's defoliating wrath.

The comb-over. This method uses the hair growth that you have on the good side of your head to cover the bad side. You let those few strands of hair grow about six feet long and before you can say "Giuliani," you're spending an hour and a half in the bathroom every morning with two mirrors and a sextant, constructing a Dairy Queen swirl ice cream cone on your head. This works fine until the first breeze hits your baldy bean and your hair unwinds and gets snagged in the spokes of a passing Harley.

Hair paint. Hey, the day I paint my head is the day I need to.

Rogaine. Even if it works for you, if you want to keep your hair, you can

never stop using it. Rogaine is the middle-aged equivalent of crack.

Hair plugs. This is where they use donor sites from one spot on your body and transplant them to your head, which is a gradual process that eventually makes you look like a postnuclear Chia pet.

Plugs can cost up to $20,000 and they look about as natural as a cornfield on a hockey rink.

And lastly, the toupee. Wearing a toupee is like covering up a carpet stain with a Day-Glo bean bag chair. My favorite faux hair faux pas is the guy with natural red hair who buys the jet black toupee. It makes his head look like the high water mark on the side of a cargo ship. Guys, trust me. There is no toupee in the world that cannot be spotted by a near-sighted mole with his back turned.

Now, there are all these euphemisms for toupees. Natural hair integration, hair replacement system, follicular restoration placement. Cut to the chase. Why don't we just call them Everybody Knows There's a Fur Divot on Your Head.

And the *crème de la crème* rinse of toupees is Sammy Donaldson. Sam Donaldson. What is it that possesses Sam to sport a rug that wouldn't be more obvious if Ali Baba was flying on it?

You know, you're damn right there's a cover-up in Washington, Sam. And it's sitting right on your Vulcan spin-art skull. Okay? Quite frankly, I can't even pay attention to what you're saying anymore because I keep waiting for that thing on the top of your head to get up on its hind legs and beg for a peanut.

Of course, that's just my opinion, I could be wrong.

AN eighty-year-old couple goes to see their doctor because they are having trouble remembering things. The doctor gives them a clean bill of health and suggests they start writing themselves little notes as reminders. The couple thank the doctor and go home.

That night, while watching TV, the old man gets up to go to the kitchen for a glass of milk. His wife asks him to bring her back a slice of apple pie and gently suggests, "Don't you think you should write it down so you remember?"

"No," he replies, "I can remember that."

"Well," she then says, "I would also like some whipped cream on top. You had better write that down because I know you'll forget."

But he says stubbornly, "I can remember that, you want a slice of apple pie with whipped cream on top," and stomps off to the kitchen.

When he returns twenty minutes later, he hands her a plate of bacon and eggs. She stares at the plate for a moment and says, "You forgot my toast."

AT a nursing home a group of seniors are sitting around the lounge complaining about their various ailments.

"My arms have gotten so weak I can hardly lift this cup of coffee," laments one of them.

"Oh, I know," says another. "My cataracts are so bad I can't even see my coffee."

"Well, I couldn't even mark an 'X' on the ballot when I went to vote last week, my hands are so crippled," offers a third.

"What? Did you say something? Speak up! I can't hear you!" says a fourth.

"Ooh, my neck is so stiff I can't

even turn my head," says a fifth, and the others nod weakly in agreement.

"My medications make me so light-headed, sometimes I can hardly walk!" declares another.

"I often forget where I am AND where I'm going," chimes in an elderly gent.

"I guess that's the price we pay for getting old," sighs an old man as he slowly shakes his head.

"Well, count your blessings," says one old lady brightly. "Thank God we can all still drive!"

TWO old ladies have been bridge partners for almost ten years. One day, during their weekly game of cards, one of the women suddenly looks up at the other and says, "I realize we've known each other for a long time, but for the life of me, I just can't bring it to mind... Would you please tell me your name again, dear?"

There is dead silence for a couple of minutes, then the other lady finally responds, "How soon do you need to know?"

You know you're getting old when getting lucky means you find your car in the parking lot.

My folks were English… we were too poor to be British. I left England at the age of four when I found out I couldn't be king. I came from a very big family. Four of us slept in the same bed. When we got cold, mother threw on another brother. I grew up with six brothers. That's how I learned to dance—waiting for the bathroom. With so many boys, my father bought us a dachshund so we could all pet him at the same time. I was well on my way to being a juvenile delinquent. When I was 16, I had more hubcaps than General Motors. I do benefits for all religions—I'd hate to blow the hereafter on a technicality. Looking at their new baby the mother said, "Those tiny little arms, he'll never be a boxer. Those tiny little legs, he'll never be a runner." The father said, "He'll never be a porn star either." You know you are getting old when the candles cost more than the cake.

Bob Hope

No performer traveled so far—and so often—to entertain so many as legendary comedian Bob Hope (1903-2003). A huge hit in Hollywood in the 1940s and 1950s, Hope rose to become one of the industry's top ten box office stars. His celebrity-packed TV specials showcased his quick wit, and included many musical numbers and classic comedy sketches. Over the course of his career, Hope received three honorary Academy Awards for his "contribution to the laughter of the world," and was even knighted by Elizabeth II, queen of his native England. The favorite performer of a string of U.S. presidents beginning with Franklin D. Roosevelt, Hope was famous for his patriotism and often traveled abroad to entertain America's troops.

Middle age is when your age starts to show around your middle.

I love to go to Washington, if only to be nearer my money. The Vietnam War finally ended in an agreement neither side intended to honor. It was like one of Zsa Zsa Gabor's weddings. I've always had a way with women… their way. If you watch a game, it's fun. If you play it, it's recreation. If you work at it, it's golf. I'm so old they've cancelled my blood type. I don't feel old. I don't feel anything till noon. That's when it's time for my nap. If I had my life to live over… I wouldn't have time.

Arthur

There was an old man of Calcutta,
Who coated his tonsils with butta,
Thus converting his snore
From a thunderous roar
To a soft, oleaginous mutta.

—Ogden Nash

Changes in the Memory After Fifty

Steve Martin

Bored? Here's a way the over-fifty set can easily kill off a good half hour:

1. Place your car keys in your right hand.
2. With your left hand, call a friend and confirm a lunch or dinner date.
3. Hang up the phone.
4. Now look for your car keys.

(For answer, turn the page and turn book upside down.)

The lapses of memory that occur after fifty are normal and in some ways beneficial. There are certain things it's better to forget, like the time Daddy once failed to praise you and now, forty years later, you have to count the tiles in the bathroom—first in multiples of three, then in multiples of five, and so on—until they come out even, or else you can't get out of the shower. The memory is selective, and sometimes it will select 1956 and 1963 and that's all. Such memory lapses don't necessarily indicate a more serious health problem. The rule is, if you think you have a pathological memory problem, you probably don't. In fact, the most serious indicator is when you're convinced you're fine and yet people sometimes ask you, "Why are you here in your pajamas at the Kennedy Center Honors?"

Let's say you've just called your best friend, Joe, and invited him to an upcoming birthday party, and then, minutes later, you call him back and invited him to the same party again. This does not mean you are "losing it" or "not playing with a full deck" or "not all there," or that you're "eating with the dirigibles" or "shellacking the waxed egg" or "looking inside your own mind and finding nothing there," or any of the demeaning epithets that are said about people who are peeling an empty banana. It does, however, mean that perhaps Joe is no longer on the list of things you're going to remember. This is Joe's fault. He should have a more memorable name, such as *El Elegante*.

Sometimes it's fun to sit in your garden and try to remember your dog's name. Here's how: Simply watch the ears while calling out pet names at random. This is a great summer activity, especially in combination with Name That Wife and Who Am I? These games actually strengthen the memory and make it simpler to solve such complicated problems as "Is this the sixth time I've urinated this hour or the seventh?" This, of course, is easily answered by tiny pencil marks applied during the day.

Note to self: Write article about waxy buildup.

If you have a doctor who is over fifty, it's wise to pay attention to his changing memory profile. There is nothing more disconcerting than patient and healer staring at each other across an examining table, wondering why they're there. Watch out for the stethoscope being placed on the forehead or the briefcase. Watch out for greetings such as "Hello…you." Be concerned if while looking for your file he keeps referring to you as "one bad boy." Men should be wary if, while examining your prostate, the doctor suddenly says, "I'm sorry, but do I know you?"

There are several theories that explain memory problems of advancing age. One is that the brain is full: It simply has too much data to compute. Easy to understand if you realize that the name of your third grade teacher is still occupying space, not to mention the lyrics to "Volare." One solution for older men is to take all the superfluous data swirling around in the brain and download it into the newly large stomach, where there is plenty of room. This frees the brain to house relevant information, like the particularly troublesome days of the week. Another solution is to take regular doses of ginkgo biloba, an extract from a tree in Asia whose memory is so indelible that one day it will hunt down and kill all the humans that have been eating it. It is strongly advised that if taking ginkgo biloba, one should label the bottle "Memory Pills." There is nothing more embarrassing than looking at a bottle of ginkgo biloba and thinking it's a reliquary for a Spanish explorer.

So in summary, waxy buildup is a problem facing all of us. Only a good strong cleanser, used once or twice a month, will save us the humiliation of that petrified yellow crust on our furniture. Again, I recommend an alcohol-free, polymer-base cleanser, applied with a damp cloth. Good luck!

[The car keys are in your right hand. Please remember to turn the book right side up.]

Three women die together in a car accident and go to heaven. When they get arrive at the pearly gates, St. Peter says, "We only have one rule here in heaven: Don't step on the ducks!"

So they enter heaven, and sure enough, there are ducks all over the place. Although they try their best to avoid them, within just a few minutes, the first woman accidentally steps on a duck.

Along comes St. Peter with the ugliest man she ever saw.

St. Peter chains the man to her and says, "Your punishment for stepping on a duck is to spend eternity chained to this ugly man!"

The next day, the second woman trips and steps on a duck and along comes St. Peter, with another extremely ugly man. He chains them together with the same admonishment he gave to the first woman.

The third woman has observed all this and, wishing to avoid the horrible fate of her friends, is very, VERY careful where she steps.

She manages to go months without stepping on any ducks, but one day St. Peter comes up to her with the most handsome man she has ever laid eyes on. And without a word, St. Peter chains them together.

The woman is overjoyed and exclaims, "I wonder what I did to deserve being chained to you for all of eternity?"

The guy says, "I don't know about you, but I stepped on a duck!"

Three men die and go to heaven. Upon their arrival, St. Peter asks the first if he was faithful to his wife. The man admits to two affairs during his marriage. St. Peter tells him that he can receive only a compact car to drive in heaven.

Then St. Peter asks the second man if he was faithful to his wife and the man admits to one affair. St. Peter tells him he will be given a midsize car to drive.

The third man is asked about his faithfulness, and he tells St. Peter he was true to his wife until the day he died. St. Peter praises him and gives him a luxury car.

A week later the three men are driving around, and they all stop at a red light. The men in the compact and midsize cars turn to see the man in the luxury car crying. They ask him what could possibly be the matter—after all, he is driving a luxury car.

"I just passed my wife," he tells them, "and she was on a skateboard."

An elderly couple get into a terrible car accident driving home one night and are both killed. They arrive in heaven and find it to be a beautiful lush golf course with a lovely clubhouse and fabulous greens. What's more, it is free and only for them.

The husband is beside himself with happiness, and asks his wife eagerly, "You want to play a round?"

She says, "Sure." And they tee off on the first hole. After his first swing the husband suddenly grows angry and throws down his club.

"What's wrong?" asks his wife.

He says, "You know, I just realized, if it hadn't been for all your stupid oat bran, we could have been here years ago!"

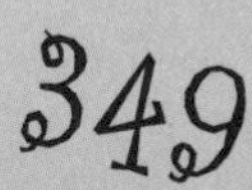

Heaven &

Heaven is a place where:
The lovers are Italian.
The cooks are French.
The mechanics are German.
The police are English.
The government is run by the Swiss.

Hell
Hell is a place where:
The lovers are Swiss.
The cooks are English.
The mechanics are French.
The police are German.
The government is run by the Italians.

ACKNOWLEDGEMENTS

LITERATURE: From *Don't Stand Too Close to a Naked Man* by Tim Allen. Copyright © 1994 Tim Allen. Reprinted by permission of Hyperion. From *Milton Berle's Private Joke File* by Milton Berle, copyright © 1989 by Milton Berle. Used by permission of Crown Publishers, a division of Random House, Inc. From *The Letters of John Cheever* edited by Benjamin Cheever. Copyright © 1988 by Benjamin Cheever. Reprinted with the permission of Simon & Schuster. From *My Point...And I Do Have One* by Ellen DeGeneres. Illustrated by Susan Rose, copyright (c) 1995 by Crazy Monkey, Inc. Illustrations (c) 1995 by Susan Rose. Used by permissions of Bantam Books, a division of Random House, Inc. From *Oh, The Things I Know!* by Al Franken, copyright © 2002 by Al Franken. Used by permission of Dutton, a division of Penguin Group (USA) Inc. From *Book* by whoopi goldberg. Copyright © 1997 by Whoopi Goldberg. Reprinted by permission of HarperCollins Publishers Inc.William Morrow. From *Social Studies* by Fran Lebowitz, copyright © 1981 by Fran Lebowitz. Used by permission of Random House, Inc. From *David Letterman's New Book of Top Ten Lists and Wedding Dress Patterns for the Husky Bride* by David Letterman, copyright © 1996 by Worldwide Pants, Inc. Used by permission of Bantam Books, a division of Random House, Inc. From *Pure Drivel* by Steven Martin. Copyright © 1998 by Steve Martin. Reprinted by permission of Hyperion. From *I Rant Therefore I Am* by Dennis Miller, copyright © 2000 by Dennis Miller. Used by permission of Doubleday, a division of Random House, Inc. "Arthur" Copyright © 1935 by Ogden Nash, renewed. Reprinted by permission of Curtis Brown, Ltd. "The Common Cold" Copyright ©1935 by Ogden Nash, renewed. Reprinted by permission of Curtis Brown, Ltd. "The Cow" Copyright ©1931 by Ogden Nash, renewed. Reprinted by permission of Curtis Brown, Ltd. "Reflections on Ice Breaking" Copyright ©1930 by Ogden Nash, renewed. Reprinted by permission of Curtis Brown, Ltd. "What's the Use?" Copyright ©1940 by Ogden Nash, renewed. Reprinted by permission of Curtis Brown, Ltd. "Symptom Recital", "Bohemia", from *Dorothy Parker: Complete Poems* by Dorothy Parker, copyright © 1999 by The National Association for the Advancement of Colored People. Used by permission of Penguin, a division of Penguin Putnam (USA) Inc. From *Rock This!* by Chris Rock. Copyright © 1997 Chris Rock. Reprinted by permission of Hyperion. From *The Complete Poems of Theodore Roethke* by Theodore Roethke, copyright 1939 by Theodore Roethke. Used by permission of Doubleday, a division of Random House, Inc. From *Everything and a Kite* by Ray Romano, copyright © 1998 by Luckykids, Inc. Used by permission of Bantam Books, a division of Random House, Inc. From Seinlanguage. Copyright © 1993 by Jerry Seinfeld. Reprinted by permission of the Author. "The Crocodile's Toothache" by Shel Silverstein. Copyright © 1974 by Evil Eye Music, Inc. *E.B. White to the ASPCA* from *"Two Letters, Both Open" From the Second Tree from the Corner* by E.B. White. Copyright © 1951 by E.B. White. Reprinted by permission of HarperCollins Publishers Inc.

ART: Parrish, Maxfield. Alphabet (School Days), 1909. Oil on board. 22" x 16" Private Collection. Photo from the archives of Alma Gilbert. Used with permission. Printed by permission of the Norman Rockwell Family Agency. Copyright © 1939 the Norman Rockwell Family Entities. "The Crocodile's Toothache" by Shel Silverstein. Copyright © 1974 by Evil Eye Music, Inc.

ILLUSTRATIONS: FRONT/BACK COVER, p. 144, 247, 283, 298: C.V. Dwiggins; p. 1, 94, 152, 162, 268, 296: Tom Browne; p. 9: Benjamin Ratier; p. 13: George Carlson; p. 19, 65, 143, 229: Carmichael; p. 26: Oliver Herford; p. 46, 241: Arthur Moreland; p. 52, 98, 127: Lawson Wood; p. 67: Chenet; p. 77, 230: Lance Thackeray; p. 79: K.M. Glackews; p. 80: Robert O'Neil; p. 90, 319: Walter Munson; p. 100: Gilette; p. 103: A.H.; p. 106: Paul Stahr; p. 110: Maxfield Parrish; p. 114: F.S. Backus; p. 122 and 123: S.W. Barrows & Co.; p. 128, 271: R. Kaplan; p. 131: Curt Teich & Co., Inc.; p. 156: R. Dillo; p. 161: Clay and Richmond; p. 176: Gustav Michelson; p. 190: Gordon Ross; p. 191: Victor C. Anderson; p. 194: H. Cowham; p.198: C. Twifrelees; p. 215: Norman Rockwell; p. 220: W.A.; p. 259, 273: E. Curtis; p. 262, 350: Gustaf Tenggren; p. 266: R.F. Outeault; p. 280: G.A.T.; p. 287: Louis Wain; p. 291: Shel Silverstein; p. 300: HBG; p. 309: Benjamin Ratier; p. 315: D.R.; p. 317: T.N.; p. 318: J.D. Cardinell; p. 334: Paul Berdanier; p. 339: H.B.G.; p. 349: Kearfote.